# No Sympathy

Chris had noticed Brenda was upset. Bart, too. But Brad seemed to be oblivious.

Woody ignored Brad's comment and turned again to Brenda. "When you get to college, you'll be twice the pro Brad is at surviving."

Everyone laughed, and Brenda's cheeks flushed crimson. "*If* I get to college," she said in a clear but shaky voice.

Brenda suddenly couldn't hold it in anymore. She looked directly at Brad and cried, "According to Mr. McQuarrie, I'm not even going to graduate, let alone go to college next year. He kept me after class to tell me I'm pretty close to failing." She looked up and met Brad's eyes, expecting some sympathy. Brad just stood there, a surprised expression on his face. He didn't say a word.

# COUPLES

Books from Scholastic
in the **Couples** series:

# BYE BYE LOVE

M.E. Cooper

SCHOLASTIC INC.
New York Toronto London Auckland Sydney

ISBN 0-590-40792-9

12 11 10 9 8 7 6 5 4 3 2 1       7 8 9/8 0 1 2/9

Printed in the U.S.A.                01

First Scholastic printing, June 1987

# Chapter
# 1

It was a hot day in early June in Rose Hill, Maryland. A *perfect* beach day, Brenda Austin thought, unsnapping the front of her lab coat and lifting her long dark hair off the back of her neck. Even with the windows wide open, Kennedy High's science building felt like an oven. A fly circled a beaker of smelly liquid bubbling over a Bunsen burner. Brenda halfheartedly batted at it, then looked back down at her lab book, pretending to work. Her mind was about a million miles away from Mr. McQuarrie's last-period chemistry lab. While her partner, fellow senior Bart Einerson, carefully adjusted the flame of the burner, Brenda doodled her boyfriend Brad's name in the margin of her notebook. In a few minutes, when class was over, she'd see him.

He'd been home from Princeton on summer vacation for two weeks now, and this afternoon Kennedy's former student body president was giving a talk to the juniors and seniors about college survival tactics. Brenda was curious about what Brad had to say, and she felt proud the school had invited him back for the talk. But she wished the meeting were some other day so they could just head off somewhere at three o'clock and be alone. She had some really good news and wanted Brad to be the first to know.

She propped her chin in her hands and tried to picture how Brad would react when she told him about her talk with Tony Martinez, the youth counselor and director of Garfield House, the local halfway house for D.C. area teens. Brad would be so proud of her. When Brenda had first moved to Rose Hill, she'd been pretty mixed up and upset by her mother's marriage to her stepfather. One cold rainy April night about two years ago, Brenda had run away and somehow landed at Garfield House. What had seemed like the end of everything had been a new beginning, and Brenda had come a long way since then. Now she worked evenings and after school at Garfield counseling other kids with problems worse than any she had ever had herself. Tony had even promised her a real job at Garfield after graduation. During college it would just be for summers and over vacations, but after college it would be full-time, actually helping him run what had turned into Washington's most successful youth center.

A hand lightly tapped Brenda's thin shoulder. She looked up, startled, into her teacher's eyes.

"Brenda?" Mr. McQuarrie said. Brenda awkwardly covered her doodles with her right arm and flushed crimson.

"Uh — " she stammered, not knowing what to say.

Mr. McQuarrie's voice was soft. Besides Brenda, only Bart overheard him. "I'd like to talk to you after class. You can both start cleaning up now." No sooner had he spoken than the bell rang, and the stuffy chemistry lab came to life in a flurry of conversation, tinkling glass, and running water.

For a moment Brenda stood still, watching the good-looking chemistry teacher head back to his desk. He had sounded so serious that Brenda felt a prickle of fear course down her spine. What had she done wrong now? Except for cutting class last week during Senior Skip Day, she couldn't think of a thing. She relaxed slightly and began rinsing out the glassware and pipettes. Skip Day, yes, that was probably it. McQuarrie was the type of teacher to really hate a school tradition like Skip Day, when all Kennedy seniors cut classes en masse to head for an amusement park or to go to the beach. Most of the faculty good-naturedly tolerated end-of-year senior antics. A few didn't. McQuarrie was probably one of those. Brenda smiled to herself. After all, as her stepsister, Chris, had said recently, the last semester of senior year was just a ritual. The teachers knew it; the students knew it. Everyone's college plans were set, and the last two months of high school were a time for partying, cementing special friendships, and looking forward to the start of a brand-new life. It was a life Brenda couldn't wait to begin.

"What was that all about?" Bart wondered aloud, nodding his head in the teacher's direction and carefully dumping the remains of their experiment down the sink. "Do you think it has something to do with cutting classes last Thursday? One of the juniors told me he threw a pop quiz and was really grumpy about us not being here," he added.

Bart's comment reassured Brenda somewhat, although McQuarrie had asked only her to stay after class, not Bart. Of course, Bart was a straight-A chem student, and Brenda had been struggling all semester to maintain a C. She shrugged and rolled her large brown eyes expressively. "Well, guess I'll find out soon enough." Then a wide smile spread across her serious face. "But to tell you the truth, *I don't care!*" She pulled off her lab coat and rolled it up into a small ball. Stuffing it into her book bag, she gave it a final satisfying punch. "I don't care, because chemistry is FINISHED, OVER, DONE WITH!!! No more chem lab for the rest of my life, and after next week, no more chemistry, period. Ever, ever again." She pushed the thin strap of her black tank top up on her shoulder and looked Bart right in the eye, declaring exultantly, "It's over. It's finally over."

Bart looked up from his lab book and chuckled. "Geez, you don't have to look that happy about it. I kind of thought you enjoyed making chemistry with me these sultry Thursday afternoons," he said in an exaggerated version of his native Montana drawl.

4

"Come off it, Bart." Brenda laughed and lightly bopped him on the head with her notebook. In spite of having a girl friend, dark-haired, blue-eyed Bart was Kennedy High's most notorious campus flirt, a fact that used to annoy Brenda to no end. But thanks to his switching lab sections this semester and ending up as her partner, she had gotten a chance to know the softhearted boy behind the Casanova facade. Now she counted him among her better friends, and without him — well, she would never have made it through Mr. McQuarrie's killer course. She shoved her long, dark hair out of her eyes, and her face turned serious as she said gratefully, "Without you and your science know-how I'm not sure I would have survived chemistry at all. It's been torture — sheer torture — and I'm so glad it's finally over."

"It's hard to believe, but in exactly two weeks *everything* will be over. Graduation's finally here," Bart said wistfully as he folded his lab coat and checked the table one last time before zipping his backpack.

Brenda sounded almost jubilant as she corrected Bart. "Graduation begins in exactly fifteen days, twelve hours, twenty minutes, and ten seconds. Then high school is over and done with — at last." She hugged her arms to her chest and gave a contented sigh.

"Aren't you going to miss it just a little?" Bart asked as the class began to file out of the room.

Brenda started shaking her head, but when she looked up at Bart and saw the sad expression in his deep blue eyes, her own eyes filled with sympathy. She patted his arm and said quietly,

5

"Don't forget, come September I'm not leaving the guy I love behind. When college starts, I'll be living just a couple of hours away from Brad. It's different for you and Holly. Too bad she's just a junior."

"Yeah," Bart acknowledged sadly. "It's going to be tough being so far away from her next year. Still, you and Brad seem to have weathered his first year away at college pretty well, and that gives me hope. I've really never had much faith in long-distance romances. And Montana is a long way from Kennedy High."

Brenda could only agree with that and silently thanked her lucky stars things were still working out between Brad and her, even after his first year at Princeton. Not having him around except for vacations had been pretty rough. But when he had come back to Rose Hill a couple of weeks ago, their relationship had seemed better than ever — in spite of the changes. Brenda smiled to herself. Yes, there had been changes. College had made a man out of Brad, and she liked that, though at first, each time she looked up into his face, she felt confused. Sometimes she wasn't quite sure that this handsome, square-faced guy was the same boy she'd said good-bye to last August. Brad looked older and actually seemed more sure of himself than before, more determined to succeed. He had made the dean's list two semesters straight, and Brenda was proud of the way he was thriving at college.

But something was definitely different between them, and Brenda couldn't quite put her finger on it. She couldn't even tell if it had to do with

Brad or her or if it was bad or good. Being with him, hanging out at the sub shop or anywhere around Rose Hill felt different than it had before he had gone away to college, and she had no idea why. Not that it seemed to matter much. As Bart had said, they had weathered the separation, and Brenda knew in her heart that their love was stronger for it.

"Where's the meeting?" Bart asked as he headed for the door. Brenda started toward the teacher's desk.

"At the Playhouse. Brad and Chris thought it would be less formal that way," Brenda replied, then added, "Hey, save me a seat, will you? Brad'll kill me if I'm not sitting front-row center!"

"For you," Bart winked, "I'll save the best seat in the house." Lowering his voice, he added, "Good luck," rolling his eyes in the teacher's direction.

Brenda nodded gratefully and let out a deep breath before facing Mr. McQuarrie. She met his eyes with a shy, questioning smile.

Perched on the edge of one of the lab tables, wearing black jeans and hightops, the dark-haired young man looked more like a rock star than Kennedy High's toughest chemistry teacher. When he didn't smile back at Brenda, she got a familiar sinking feeling in the pit of her stomach, the kind of feeling she'd had constantly her first few months at Kennedy when she was always in trouble for cutting classes or goofing off. Brenda hadn't cut a class or gotten detention for over a year now, and neither she nor any of her teachers thought of her as one of the problem kids anymore. Her involvement with Garfield had gained her the respect of students and teachers alike around the quad. Still, from the look on Mc-Quarrie's face right now she could see something was really wrong, and she couldn't imagine what. She swallowed hard. Though she instinctively liked McQuarrie's honest, no-nonsense manner, talking one-on-one with any of her teachers still made her feel vaguely nervous and defensive.

As he cleared his throat, Brenda glanced up at the clock. Brad's talk to the juniors and seniors about how to survive your first year at college was scheduled to start in ten minutes. With a little luck Brenda would make it to the Playhouse just in time.

"I won't beat around the bush," Mr. McQuarrie said, looking directly at Brenda and drumming his fingers against the black stone tabletop. "I know chemistry is not your favorite subject."

Though his tone was straightforward and not at all sarcastic, Brenda cringed slightly and tightened her grip on the looseleaf notebook she held against her chest.

"But," he continued, "it is a required course here at Kennedy. Most students take it junior year, but transfer students like you and Bart often don't get a chance until you're seniors."

Brenda forced herself to take a couple of deep breaths. Something about McQuarrie's attitude was making her very nervous. Whatever he had to say, she wished he would get it over and done with — quickly.

"Unfortunately, when you're a senior, there's no chance to take it again."

"Take it again?" Brenda repeated. Her stomach did a double somersault. "I — I don't understand."

"Brenda," Mr. McQuarrie said gently. "Did you even look at the last two quizzes I handed back?"

Brenda winced. "I haven't had a chance yet. I — "

Before she could explain about her heavy counseling schedule at Garfield House, Mr. McQuarrie interrupted. "I know. June of your senior year is a very busy time: graduation rehearsals, parties, dinners. But Brenda, unless you pull at least a C in your final, you are going to fail chemistry."

Brenda's mouth fell open. "Fail?"

Her teacher nodded. "You failed your last two quizzes, and your grades haven't exactly been high all semester. Unfortunately, as I said, chemistry is a required course. If you fail — you can't graduate."

Brenda took a quick step backward. She felt as if she had just been kicked in the stomach. She stood speechless for only an instant. "Mr. McQuarrie!" she finally cried. "You can't mean that. You can't fail me in chemistry." She looked frantically around the empty lab, wishing someone were there to stand up for her, to help her state her case, or to tell her she was dreaming.

Not graduating. The words rolled around in her head, making her dizzy. Two years ago she would have said she couldn't have cared less. But now — now everything had changed. She had worked so hard at everything — her schoolwork, accepting her new family, working out her hostility, trying to do her best at whatever she tackled. Graduating meant more to her now than almost anything. "Mr. McQuarrie, I've already been accepted to college. This is the last semester of senior year!" she cried, then said in a low, shaky voice, "You can't fail me now. You just can't."

"Brenda, I'm not going to fail you in chemistry. It's up to you, not me, to pass or fail. And you won't fail if you buckle down and study. I know it's a lot of pressure this time of year, with all the senior activities going on and end-of-the-year excitement, but if I didn't think you could pass the final with at least a C, I'd tell you so now."

The teacher stood up and walked to the long demonstration table at the front of the room. He straightened some papers in a manila folder. When he looked back up at Brenda, his face was filled with concern. "Brenda, I know you're not a science whiz. Your talents, and you are talented," he emphasized, "lie in other directions. But as unconnected as it may seem now, passing chemistry, and doing your best at it, has a lot to do with working with people. Knowing you have succeeded yourself at something you think you can't do will help you tell other kids that they can do the same. No?" He studied Brenda's face carefully.

Brenda wasn't listening. She stared down at the gray tiled floor, a sullen expression darkening her uncommonly beautiful face. She couldn't believe it. Just ten minutes ago she had been happy and relieved that she had made it through this dreaded course. Now, passing chemistry seemed out of the question. So did graduation. Angry, hurt feelings roiled inside her. She suddenly felt trapped.

She tossed her hair back with a defiant gesture but didn't meet her teacher's eye. Part of her just wanted to bolt out of the laboratory onto the quad and run all the way home. On second thought, she didn't want to go home. She'd go somewhere where she didn't have to face her parents; her stepsister, Chris; and her friends again. Just the idea of not graduating was so humiliating. Two little red spots began to burn on her cheeks. She felt like lashing out at McQuarrie. She'd show him. She'd run away and not bother to show up for his idiotic final. Besides, she told herself, he would probably fail her now, anyway, no matter how well she did on that crummy test. She couldn't think of one case where a kid had gotten a warning from a teacher and ended up passing a course. She might as well give up now and save herself and her teacher the trouble of pretending she could salvage what was surely a lost cause.

"Brenda?" Mr. McQuarrie's voice was very gentle.

Brenda let out a sigh and bit the inside of her lip. Slowly the wave of anger and fear subsided, leaving her scared and vulnerable. The soft lilt of Mr. McQuarrie's voice reminded her of her friend Tony, and the thought of Tony and Garfield calmed her down. She imagined how Tony would talk to her now if this were a session at Garfield House. Whenever something tough happened, he would point out, Brenda automatically went into a panic and withdrew from reality: the demands and details of the tough situation.

Brenda forced her thoughts to slow down, and immediately the situation came into focus. This discussion about chemistry wasn't the end of the world. It was simply some bad news that she could — no, she *had* to — deal with. All Mr. McQuarrie had really said was that she had to study very hard for her final. If she studied, she would pass.

Brenda shifted her books to her hip. McQuarrie wasn't telling her something she didn't know already. The past month or so she had hardly cracked a book. She'd been too caught up with her work at Garfield House and all the senior activities at school. Obviously her chemistry grades were showing the strain.

She took a couple more deep breaths. When she looked up, she met her teacher's gaze head-on. "I'll try, Mr. McQuarrie. I'll try to do it," she said. The words sounded like they were coming over some long-distance phone connection rather than from her own throat. Brenda gritted her teeth and corrected herself in a firm, strong voice. "I mean, I'll do it. I'll pass the test." To herself she added, I've got to.

# Chapter
# 2

Brenda arrived at the Playhouse just in time to see Laurie Bennington's red miniskirt vanish inside the front door. "Ooooh, I must be really late," she muttered. Laurie was famous for late entrances. Though she was already panting from her run across the quad in the ninety-degree heat, Brenda doubled her pace and tore up the steps of the old colonial-style chapel that served as Kennedy's campus theater.

She entered the hall from the side door and paused to catch her breath. Her talk with her teacher had left her feeling off balance. She had meant what she'd said about passing the test. She would do it. *How* she'd do it was another matter. McQuarrie took it for granted that Brenda's study problems had to do with too much graduation partying. Brenda only wished they did. Skipping parties to study would be a drag, but she'd do it. Skipping counseling sessions at Garfield was impossible, especially since, at the moment, she was responsible for a particularly difficult runaway. Brenda stood with her hand on the door frame, taking one deep breath after another, trying to calm down.

No matter how hot it was outside, the Little Theater always seemed to hoard bits of winter under it eaves, and the cool, musty air felt good on her bare back and shoulders. As soon as her eyes adjusted to the dim light, she instinctively looked toward the stage and Brad. The instant she saw him, the distracted nervous sensation inside her eased up. Brad had his back against the podium, his hands stuffed in the pockets of his light-colored slacks, his face intensely focused on someone three or four rows back asking a question. His striped shirt was slightly rumpled from the heat, and his sleeves were rolled up. In one hand he held a soda, but otherwise he looked very much the part of a young Ivy League professor giving a lecture. It was hard to believe just a year ago he'd stood in the same spot as outgoing student body president, giving the same sort of emotional farewell speech that Brenda's stepsister, Chris, had been busy preparing over the past week.

Brenda only wished his talk were over, and she could steal off somewhere alone with him and shed some of the tears that were building behind her eyes. Once in Brad's arms, she knew the feelings of insecurity and fear would vanish. In a matter of minutes he'd have her laughing at herself. You could always depend on Brad to be sensible and calm, no matter what was going on.

He'd help her figure out a good study schedule. He'd make everything seem possible. That was one reason Brenda loved him. Brad believed you could do anything you wanted, provided you wanted it badly enough. Just being near him steadied her, and she definitely needed his steadiness now.

True to his promise, Bart had saved her a front-row seat between Chris and himself. Brenda pushed aside the temptation to slip unobserved into an empty seat by the door, and instead tiptoed down the side aisle just as everyone burst into a round of raucous laughter. Apparently Brad had just said something very funny. Though she hadn't heard the joke, Brenda found herself smiling, too, as she plopped down next to Chris.

Chris brushed a stray strand of blonde hair off her forehead and whispered, "You okay?"

Brenda's body stiffened. She hadn't realized she looked as upset as she felt. She forced herself to relax and willed the tension out of her neck and shoulders. She shook her head no and whispered back, "I'll tell you later."

Chris's bright blue eyes searched Brenda's worried brown ones for a second, then Chris gave her sister's arm a reassuring squeeze and turned her attention back to the stage.

In spite of Brad's soothing voice resounding through the auditorium, Chris's reaction to her set Brenda on edge. Sitting here next to Chris and listening to Brad talk about success, the possibility of not graduating suddenly seemed more awful than ever. How could she ever face her family again if she couldn't graduate? It was too awful to think about. Over the last couple of years Brenda had gradually stopped thinking of Chris as the good, successful sister and herself as the bad one, a born loser. But it would be pretty hard to convince her stepfather that she was no longer the black sheep of the Austin family if on graduation day Chris was class valedictorian and Brenda was the only senior of her crowd not wearing a cap and gown.

"Hey, Bren, what happened with McQuarrie?" Bart said under his breath. Holly Daniels, sitting on Bart's other side leaned forward, too.

"He's a pill, isn't he? I really lucked out when I got Ms. Barish for chemistry this semester," Holly whispered.

Slumping down in her seat, Brenda didn't exactly lie as she replied, "It was nothing. Something about an exam." Brenda wasn't sure she was ready for everyone in the world to know the gory details of the latest crisis in the life of Brenda Austin. To silence Holly and Bart, she put a finger to her lips and nodded toward the stage.

Brad was looking in her direction. When he caught her glance, he gave her a quick but intimate smile. A bolt of warmth shot through Brenda, giving her courage. She sat up straighter to hear what he was saying. If she paid attention to Brad right now, she wouldn't have to think of her own problems for the next few minutes. She propped her chin on her hands and listened very intently.

With one hand Brad slicked back his sun-streaked brown hair and smiled pleasantly as he looked around the auditorium. "When some of you hit the college campuses, you're going to think you've found the dream life. No more parents, no more curfews — none that really matter much, anyway — no one looking over your shoulder day and night saying you've got to do this or that. Those all-night parties you've heard so much about aren't just rumors — they're real!"

"Tell us about it, Davidson!" Peter Lacey yelled from the end of the row.

Brad grinned broadly, showing off his chipped front tooth. It was the one feature Brenda always kidded him about. Without that tooth Brad would have resembled some young hero on *General Hospital* — the kind of guy free-spirited Brenda couldn't imagine wanting to talk to, let alone kiss.

"They're fun, too — " Brad quipped in response. "And coed dorms really do exist. I live in one!"

A ripple of laughter and comments ran through the audience. Brad raised both arms and made a gesture for the audience to quiet down.

"I guess we'll have to pump him later about life in the coed dorms," Bart said wickedly to whoever was listening.

Brenda laughed off Bart's comment easily. She never worried about Brad in the girl department. He was definitely a one-girl guy and very loyal, but his next words bothered her, and Brenda shifted uncomfortably in her seat as he went on.

"But even with all that going on around you, you can't play harder. Because if you do, poof!" Brad snapped his fingers for emphasis. "Down

17

go the grades, down go your chances to get where you're going *after* college. Because college isn't the end, my friends, it's just the beginning. It's a stepping-stone to *real life!*" He spoke with great solemnity, then ever so slowly started grinning.

The audience reaction was predictable. Half the kids groaned, the rest of them hooted. Brenda sank down further into her seat and cursed inwardly. She felt like putting her hands over her ears. Instead she clenched them very tightly together in her lap. Today she was not in the mood to hear about *real life*, from Brad or anyone else. At the moment the real life of Brenda Austin was not a very pleasant thing to be living.

Obviously pleased with the effect he'd made, Brad continued to smile as he said, "That got your attention, didn't it." He laughed as he ducked a paper plane someone launched from the third row. He obligingly sent it back in the direction of its owner and resumed his talk. "The point is, doing well over the next four years is to your benefit. You'll be the one to get into a good med or law school. You'll be the one to land that great job. The problem with college is once you get there, everything seems to be conspiring against your doing well. Not that you can't have a good time, make some great friends, have plenty of new experiences that stretch you in directions you never dreamed of. But you've got to be the one to put on the brakes when everyone wants to party the night before the big exam. That's the secret to success — learning how to set priorities. Because failing in college means a lot more than failing Cartwell's sophomore year geometry class."

18

Brenda squirmed in her seat and tuned out the rest of Brad's speech. Everything Brad was saying made sense, but today of all days, she just wished he wouldn't talk about failing. The conviction that Brad would sympathize with her plight evaporated. Talking to Brad suddenly didn't seem like such an easy, natural thing to do. He sounded as if he thought failing something were the worst thing in the world. What would he think when he heard his own girl friend wasn't only about to fail chemistry, but actually might not graduate?

"Brenda! Over here!" Brad's voice rang out across the tiny theater lobby. Someone had propped the entrance doors open, and the crowd of well-wishers surrounding Brad spilled out the door and down the broad front steps of the building into the sun. Brenda made her way to Brad's side, wondering where all these juniors and seniors had come from. She'd been at Kennedy two years now, and she was certain she'd never seen half of these people before. Of course, Brad had been a very popular student body president, and he had made it his business to know almost every student in the school. No wonder everyone turned up.

Woody, Phoebe, Michael, Ted, and just about all of Brenda and Brad's friends were clustered around Brad, congratulating him on his talk. Brenda approached hesitantly, longing to tell him how wonderful he had been, but still feeling a bit uncomfortable about his message.

As soon as she was close enough Brad's hand

shot out for hers, and he pulled her to his side. "Was it okay?" he asked, smiling down into her troubled eyes.

"You were great, Brad. You really were," she said, pushing her own feelings aside for the moment.

Brad gave her a long, grateful look before folding her into his arms. Brenda's doubts about confiding in him disappeared. She hugged him very tightly and said, "Something really rotten happened. We've got to talk."

Brad made no move to get away from the crowd. "Later, okay?" He pecked Brenda on the cheek and resumed his conversation with Ted.

"So, Mason, what do you think of my survival hints?" Brad asked his friend as he pulled Brenda a little closer. Brenda could feel his excitement over the successful audience response to his speech. She wanted to feel happy for Brad, but at the moment she couldn't.

Ted pretended to consider Brad for a moment. "Oh, I don't know," he said very slowly. "You made it sound like a jungle out there!"

"A jungle?" Bart pushed his way up toward Brad's side. He whacked Brad on the back and said, "Where do I sign up for the safari? College sounds like fun to me. At least the college Brad goes to, right, Brenda?" he teased.

Brenda managed a thin smile and said under her breath to Brad, "I'm serious. Can we get out of here?"

"Uh — sure," Brad replied. "Hey, anyone game for the sub shop? All that talking sure works up a thirst."

Woody, Phoebe, Ted, and the rest of the crowd cheered Brad's suggestion. As he started down the stairs, still holding Brenda's hand, she hung back slightly. He let go of her and slung one arm around Ted, one around Peter, and began talking animatedly about an incident at school.

"Brad, I've got to talk to you, *alone!*" This time Brenda didn't bother to keep her voice down. "It's important," she cried. She couldn't believe it, but Brad didn't seem to hear.

She was standing perfectly still on top of the steps gaping at Brad in disbelief, when suddenly Woody came up behind her and slapped his huge paws on her shoulders. "So, how does it feel to have an in with Mr. Ivy League!" He guided Brenda down the steps after the rest of the crowd.

"I wouldn't know," Brenda muttered, not sure if she felt hurt or annoyed at Brad's behavior. She knew he was excited about his talk and happy to be back with all his old friends. But at the moment he was acting like a real jerk as far as she was concerned. She had told him two or three times now she needed to talk to him. It would only take a couple of minutes. But nothing was going to pull him out of the center of the crowd, the center of attention.

Brenda hurried after the others, barely listening to Woody's chatter. The group was waiting for Woody and her on the edge of the parking lot.

"Are you sure this is your boyfriend? The very same Brad Davidson who just a mere twelve months ago was a lowly senior like you and me at dear old Kennedy?" Woody said as they joined the crowd. He wriggled his bushy eyebrows and

21

pretended to look suspicious as he fingered Brad's starched collar. He lowered his voice and whispered loud enough for everyone to hear, "Watch out, Bren. Mr. Ivy League here isn't really the Brad we knew and loved. He's undercover for college recruitment. He gives these long-winded lectures, and anyone who falls asleep is axed." Woody drew his long finger across his neck and staggered a couple of steps across the pavement.

"Speak for yourself, Webster. You were snoring loud enough to wake the dead!" Brad laughed, then winked at Brenda.

Brenda just looked at him. Chris had noticed she was upset. Bart, too. But Brad seemed to be oblivious.

Woody ignored Brad's comment and turned again to Brenda. "Of course, you could afford to sleep through his talk. You probably know it all by heart now. When you get to college, you'll be twice the pro Brad is at surviving."

Everyone laughed, and Brenda's cheeks flushed crimson. "*If* I get to college," she said in a clear but shaky voice.

Chris giggled and poked her stepsister lightly in the ribs. "Come off it, Bren. You got your acceptance to Sarah Lawrence a month ago."

Brenda suddenly couldn't hold it in anymore. She looked directly at Brad and cried, "According to Mr. McQuarrie, I'm not even going to graduate, let alone go to college next year." There, it was out. Brenda kicked at the gravel with her pointy black flat and folded her arms across her chest.

Everyone fell silent. Chris grabbed Brenda's hand. "Brenda, what are you talking about?"

Brenda sighed miserably and leaned back against a car. "That's what he told me just now. That's why I was late for Brad's talk. He kept me after class to tell me I'm pretty close to failing." She looked up and met Brad's eyes, expecting some sympathy. Brad just stood there, a surprised expression on his face. He didn't say a word.

"McQuarrie's a real stinker!" Holly cried. "He can't do that to you."

"But you passed your midterm, didn't you?" Phoebe asked. When Brenda nodded, she let out a sigh and continued, "I can't believe it. He should at least pass you on principle!"

"Yeah, what's chemistry got to do with the rest of your life, anyway?" Bart commented sourly. He walked up to Brenda and put his arm around her. "Don't let him scare you. That's all he was trying to do."

"Besides, you'll pass," Chris added firmly. "I know you will."

"Hang in there, Brenda!" Peter said, and the rest of the crowd chimed in.

"Thanks for all the good wishes and stuff," Brenda said wryly, "but what I really need is at least a C in the final, or I'm done for."

"You'll just have to hit the books, I guess," Brad finally spoke up. He walked toward Brenda, his hands in his pockets. From the look on his face Brenda could tell he was disappointed, as though she had let him down somehow. She looked away.

"Well, that's pretty obvious, isn't it," she said a bit more sharply than she intended.

"But maybe he's wrong, Bren," Phoebe mused aloud.

"I do have to study, Pheeb; there's no way I can wing it through McQuarrie's chem final otherwise," Brenda said, wishing she had never blurted out her news in front of everyone. She was glad for the crowd's support, but Brad's lack of it hurt, and suddenly Brenda felt ashamed. He was making her feel as if she had already failed at something.

"I don't mean what Brad said," Phoebe explained, retying the strap on her old pink overalls. She tossed her thick red braid behind her shoulders and regarded Brenda with thoughtful green eyes. "I mean McQuarrie. Maybe chemistry isn't an absolute requirement."

"I don't know about that, Pheeb," Chris said dubiously. "Everyone has to take it."

"I know. I know." Phoebe brushed aside Chris's comment. "But Brenda should find out from the horse's mouth, before she gets more worked up about this than absolutely necessary. I'd hate to see her miss all the fun these next few weeks," Phoebe added warmly. "Why don't you ask the guidance counselor? They have your records. Believe me, Kennedy High doesn't want to have one of its seniors not graduate. I bet they can work something out."

Brenda's brow creased in a frown. She hadn't thought of that.

"Meanwhile, let's go to the sub shop and hang McQuarrie in effigy," Woody suggested, throwing

24

his arm around Brenda and pulling her toward his red Volvo.

"All right!" Peter said.

Phoebe shook her head violently. She turned to Brenda. "The counseling office is still open. I think you should head over there now. Don't wait until tomorrow. At least you'll know what the situation is before you go home."

Again Brenda sought Brad's eyes. This time he managed a rather unconvincing smile and said, "Uh, why don't you do that, Bren. You can tell me what happens later."

"Good idea," Brenda said in a quiet, controlled voice. "Thanks for the suggestion, Phoebe." Then she turned on her heel without bothering to say good-bye to anyone. She marched across the parking lot holding her head high, tears stinging her eyes. "How could he?" she muttered. Instead of supporting her, Brad had been the one friend who had held back. He hadn't said anything critical, or put her down, but he had stood there looking at her like she was some kind of freak who was too dumb to pass chemistry — a loser he couldn't believe he actually knew, let alone dated. She had the feeling if they hadn't been standing with their group of friends he would have turned away, pretended that he didn't know her.

It wasn't good for his image to be going out with a girl like her, and the message had been written all over his face.

# *Chapter*
## *3*

Phoebe Hall sat in the sub shop having another attack of the "lasts" and beginning to wonder if she was abnormal. Watching Woody clown around had never made her feel like crying before. Today Woody was in top form, sporting a fake Cyrano de Bergerac nose, pretending he was the food reviewer from a local TV station. In an accent more Frankenstein than French he pronounced one sandwich after another "A-okay," "not so good," or "zee very best!" Already Brad, Bart, and Ted had hightailed it out of the crowded after-school joint, declaring loudly that they wanted nothing to do with this raving maniac. While the rest of the gang cracked up, Phoebe sat with her chin in her hands, feeling very blue.

Her symptoms had started nearly a month ago at the prom — her *last* high school prom — when she realized for the very first time that senior year was almost over, and come graduation, Kennedy High would become part of her past. Last week had been the *last* choral club concert, the *last* drama club meeting, the *last* baseball game she'd see Ted Mason play in the red and yellow Cardinal uniform. Today had been her *last* drama seminar class with Woody, and when the imaginary curtain descended on the classroom reading of *Cyrano*, Phoebe knew a whole era of her life had ended. She and Woody had been friends ever since their seventh-grade teacher, Mrs. Merryweather, had cast them opposite each other in the junior high production of *Arsenic and Old Lace*. Now they'd never be in a play together again.

"Why so glum, Pheebarebop?" Peter leaned across the booth and gently tugged Phoebe's thick braid.

Phoebe managed a sad smile. "I'm just going to miss all this — so much!" Her voice quavered dangerously on the last two words. Hearing herself sound so woebegone, Phoebe's tentative smile gave way to a bout of hysterical giggles. She brushed away tears of laughter and exclaimed, "Am I going crazy or what?"

Several "ayes" greet her question.

"You're too much!" Chris howled from the far corner of the booth. "How could watching Woody make anyone cry?"

"It's going to make you cry!" Morty, the shop's mustachioed proprietor shouted over the general din. "Give my Salami Sinker Sub a bad review, and I'm going to slice that nose of yours into a

27

Bologna Hero!" He reached across the counter and gave Woody's red suspenders a resounding snap.

"*Mon Dieu!!!!*" Woody gasped, then staggered, then gasped again. "My nose!" He patted the long, bulbous nose affectionately, then whipped it off and tossed it behind him. It landed within inches of Sasha Jenkins's salad.

Sasha shrieked and shielded her food from the nose. "My salad — you defiled it with flesh!" she said dramatically, cracking everyone up again.

As soon as she recovered, Chris heaved a sigh and leaned her head against Greg Montgomery's arm. "I'm going to miss all this, too."

Greg tenderly stroked Chris's golden hair and cleared his throat. "Just this?" he whispered. Chris looked directly into his eyes, and the couple shared a very long, private sort of look. Chris was graduating in a couple of weeks. Greg, just a sophomore, had two more years to go at Kennedy. They were making a pretty good show of not minding the inevitable break of their relationship come September, but sometimes when they let their guard down, their friends got the impression Greg wasn't going to weather Chris's departure for New England and Mount Holyoke very well.

Phoebe cleared her throat loudly and teased her friend. "You admit it. It's not just me who has the weepies. You, too, are going to pine for our long, lazy afternoons contemplating Smokey over a half-eaten sub."

"But just think how Smokey will feel! His nearest and dearest buddies abandoning him like this!" Woody piped up and posed himself near the moth-eaten stuffed bear that was the sub shop's mascot. At the moment it sported Jonathan Preston's felt Indiana Jones hat and held a Kennedy pennant in its right paw. Someone had pinned a sheet of looseleaf to its chest. KILL MC QUARRIE was printed on it in big block letters. Everyone in the crowd had signed their name beneath the message.

"It's been absolutely ages since he's felt a thing," Laurie pointed out, jabbing the mascot in the stomach with a long, elegantly manicured fingernail. "Poor thing! He never had any fun!" She pushed aside her Diet Coke and stood up. Stretching her arms high over her head, she sighed and turned to Janie Barstow. "Speaking of fun, I'm heading for Rezato's to do some shopping for school. Want to come?"

"But it's not even summer yet — officially," Jeremy Stone said, amazed. "You can't possibly be thinking of buying clothes for college now!"

"At the University of Miami it's always summer. And I want to get my shopping done early. After all, the week after graduation I leave town for most of vacation," Laurie said coyly. Janie exchanged a glance with the other kids, but got up and followed Laurie to the door. "Henry showed his new line to Rezato's this afternoon. I want to see how it went," Janie said by way of explanation. Her boyfriend's dress design business was booming and had helped land Janie and Henry both in New York's prestigious Fashion Institute of Technology come September.

As soon as Laurie's red miniskirt vanished from sight, Peter groaned. "If I hear one more time about Laurie's upcoming fabulous summer plans, I am going to die, just die. I don't know how anyone puts up with her." The handsome Kennedy DJ buried his head in his arms and groaned again.

Monica Ford laughed. "Oh, I don't know. Speaking of missing stuff, I'm even going to miss Laurie." Peter sat bolt upright and glared at his girl friend as if she had betrayed him. Flirtatious, conniving Laurie had mellowed out over the past year or so, and most of the crowd got on with her pretty well now. Still, Peter found her more than a bit cloying. After a moment his look softened, and he admitted sheepishly, "Me, too. She was a great Candy Hearts!" He chuckled remembering Laurie's WKND stint as on-air advice-to-the-lovelorn columnist last Valentine's Day.

"You should see the picture we have of that one!" Jeremy shouted before his girl friend, Diana, clapped her hand over his mouth. "Whoops, I blew it again," Jeremy said happily. "I keep forgetting this American high school yearbook stuff is top secret."

"Only until tomorrow!" Michael Rifkin reminded him.

"Tomorrow?" Phoebe repeated. "Oh, gosh! The yearbook's coming out tomorrow, isn't it? I had forgotten all about it!" She clapped her hands delightedly.

"Tomorrow we all get our yearbooks, and all those memories will be yours to cherish forever — have I got that right?" Jeremy asked in his clipped British accent. He had memorized one of Laurie Bennington's cornier sales pitches as to why every student should buy a yearbook.

30

Michael nodded. "Perfect, Jeremy, just perfect." He hooked his hands behind his head and said thoughtfully, "But a yearbook can never capture what really went on, here in the sub shop, for instance, for the last four years."

"What do you mean, Michael?" Jonathan Preston leaned forward in his seat.

"Oh, you know. The visual gags, the awful timing of Woody's jokes — stuff like that!!"

"What — what — " Woody sputtered. "The awful *what* of my jokes. My dear man — " He whipped a cold french fry out of his plate and slipped into his Cyrano accent. "I challenge thee to a duel — though, on second thought, it eeez not worth it, *non*. I, too, wouldn't mind a yearbook that captured the moment when your out-of-tune cello played 'The Star-Spangled Banner' at assembly the time the sound system broke down."

Michael laughed good-naturedly. "Touché, Monsieur Woodeeee!"

"Why don't we do it, then?" Jeremy said.

"Do what?" Chris asked, beginning to feel very lost and wishing she were off somewhere alone with Greg, rather than in what was beginning to sound like a madhouse.

"Tape a living yearbook."

"We could interview the seniors," Karen Davis spoke up from beside Sasha Jenkins. Karen was taking over Sasha's editorial duties on *The Red and the Gold* come September and currently co-hosted WKND's popular *Newsnotes* program.

"You're serious!" Phoebe gasped. "What a crazy idea. I love it." She looked at Chris. "Imag-

31

ine seeing us the way we are now, next year, ten years from now — "

"Or when we are very, very old!" Chris faked a creaky voice. "Oh, let's do it. But do we have time, and when will we show the tapes? And can we make copies?"

"Whoa!" Jonathan tried to quiet everyone down. "I think it's a great idea, but it'll take some planning. We're all awfully busy with finals the next few weeks, and you seniors have all these graduation shindigs to go to. How would you work this, Jeremy?"

"I could start taping the interviews tomorrow. It doesn't have to be the whole class—just our crowd. What do you say, Karen?"

"I'm game," Karen enthused. "I'm free tomorrow afternoon and Saturday and a couple of afternoons next week. We could probably finish it up by next weekend."

"But where would we show it?" Woody asked.

"The Senior Class Dinner," Sasha suggested.

"That wouldn't work," Peter protested. "This is just for our closest friends, not the whole class, and the whole class will be at that dinner."

"Well, we'll just have to give our own party!" Monica said with obvious delight.

Phoebe shook her head. A wicked grin flashed across her pretty face. "Not an *ordinary* party." She caught Chris's eye. She'd need Chris's support in this, and she had a hunch she could count on it. "I think we should have a roast!"

"A roast?" Several people said in unison.

"Who are we roasting?" Woody asked, looking

around surreptitiously and covering the stuffed bear's ears. "Not Smokey, I hope?"

Everyone else looked around the table as the brilliance of Phoebe's idea dawned on them. "You, Woodrow Wilson Webster! And it's about time, too!" Phoebe's voice rang out and was followed by a chorus of cheers and whoops.

Woody turned red as a beet and sank in a mock faint against the sub shop counter.

"Let's ask Laurie if we can have the roast at her house. She has that great video system," Chris said.

"And I bet Kim will be happy to provide a roast — for the Roast!" Monica punned cheerfully.

"Speaking of roasts, I'm going to be roasted if I don't get out of here!" Phoebe wailed, checking the antique Betty Boop watch her kid brother, Shawn, had already given her for graduation. "Shawn's got aikido this afternoon, and I'm supposed to pick him up. If we're late for dinner, Mom's going to slit my throat."

"Hold up a minute," Chris cried, exchanging smiles with Sasha, then hurrying to the door to catch up with Phoebe. "I'll walk you to the car." They plunged out of the air-conditioning into the heat, and Phoebe groaned.

"Who turned summer on?"

"Really," Chris said. "Listen, Pheeb, Sasha and I were talking at lunch, and we decided it would be great to have one last great gleesome threesome sleepover before we graduate."

Phobe stopped dead in her tracks. "You mean

just you, me, and Sasha, like we used to do in junior high?"

Chris bobbed her head in agreement.

"But wouldn't Brenda feel left out — "

"I don't think so. I'll check, though. Sleepovers were probably never her style; besides she'd understand this is just for old times' sake. We can have it at Sasha's house. We'll keep it top secret, and get out old records, and eat popcorn, and rent a period movie!"

"A horror movie, a real frightening one, like the kind that used to scare you to death!" Phoebe indulged in an evil laugh. "Remember the time we — " she cut herself off from her own recollection of one slumber party when she and Sasha spooked Chris in the shower after watching *Psycho* on TV with all the lights off. "Maybe I'd better just remember the time, *period*, and get to the fitness center and Shawn before my parents get into one of their grounding modes. But yes, Chris, let's do it. Call me tonight. We can make plans then."

Phoebe climbed into her station wagon but didn't turn on the ignition right away. She rested her chin on the steering wheel and watched Chris lope down the sidewalk, her blonde hair bright with sun. When she disappeared back into the sub shop, Phoebe sighed and started the car. She was going to miss hanging out with Chris next year. Of course, Smith and Mount Holyoke weren't far from each other, and Phoebe knew in her heart Chris and she would see each other lots and always stay friends. But it wouldn't be the same. Sasha, at the University of Virginia,

34

wouldn't be anywhere nearby, and Phoebe knew Chris and Sasha must sense things would never be the same, too. Otherwise, they wouldn't be planning this special last-time-ever sleepover. College was bound to change things among them, and it wasn't a change Phoebe was looking forward to.

In fact, Phoebe thought, as she carefully pulled out into the traffic on Rosemont Boulevard, none of the changes looming ahead after graduation felt really good at all, especially with Michael going to school at Juilliard in New York while she was in the middle of Massachusetts. She only wished she could be as excited and carefree and happy about graduating as everyone else. If she could, she would stop time right now and suspend them all in this magical moment between high school and independence.

She had tried to explain her feelings to Chris at lunch last Monday — how Grad Night, Skip Day, and all the other fun end-of-year events were making her feel weird instead of great. She felt like she was looking out the rear window of a speeding car, watching familiar landmarks fade away in the distance behind her. Soon graduation, long afternoons at the sub shop with her friends, horsing around with Woody, would all be just memory. Chris had just laughed at her and said something about not looking behind but looking ahead, to see where she was going and how wonderful and promising the future would be.

As Phoebe neared the fitness center, she sniffed and rubbed the sleeve of her shirt across her nose. Maybe the future was full of adventures for Chris, but Phoebe wasn't sure she was the adventurous sort at all, especially without all her old pals around.

She had her doubts about her own future. Her plan of someday becoming a famous actress and singer was beginning to seem unrealistic. Now that someday was near at hand, her plan seemed like a crazy girlish dream, the kind of romantic stuff you thought about in high school but grew out of as soon as you were eighteen and knew better. Phoebe wasn't eighteen yet, but she was beginning to wonder if her dream was just that, a dream. And if it was, then her future looked to be full of blank spaces, and not the adventures Chris had so confidently predicted.

# Chapter
# 4

"Summer school?" Chris tried to digest what Brenda had just told her. With a dismal shake of her head, she tossed the dish towel on the counter and leaned back and regarded her stepsister. "Ugh! What an awful idea!"

"McQuarrie was right," Brenda said reaching for the large bottle of dishwashing liquid above the kitchen sink. She squeezed a liberal amount into the already sudsy water and plunged her arms in, elbow-deep. Whenever Brenda's problems seemed insurmountable, she volunteered for dish duty and, ignoring the dishwasher, scrubbed every dish by hand until it shone. It was a trick she'd learned from a kid at Garfield House. A bout of old-fashioned housework sometimes made problems easier to deal with. "I checked with the guidance counselor. If I don't pass chemistry, I don't graduate," she stated flatly. She reached for a casserole dish and began to scrub burned bits of cheese off the handles.

"Of course, Ms. Murdock was very matter-of-fact when she said lots of kids are in the same situation. They just make up the course in summer school, and it doesn't affect college admission at all. 'So, don't worry, dearie' — " Brenda gave a pretty poor imitation of the guidance counselor's notoriously squeaky voice, then mugged a disgusted face. "I hate when people call me that."

"Did you tell her that?" Chris knew what her sister would answer.

Brenda couldn't help cracking a smile. " 'Fraid so!" she said, and they both laughed. Brenda looked around the large Austin kitchen to see if there were more dishes. Finding none, she pulled the plug in the sink and propped her elbows on the stainless steel rim to watch the suds swirl down the drain. She kept her eyes focused on the water and said casually, "And in about half an hour I get to tell Brad the big news. Now that he's taken that summer construction job so we'd have more time together, I'm sure he'll be thrilled to hear that I'll be in summer school. I can just picture his reaction!" Brenda's voice was slightly bitter.

Chris stopped drying the casserole and considered her sister carefully. "What do you mean, Bren? Don't jump to conclusions. You may not be going to summer school at all. I think you're going to pull a C on that test. In fact, I *know* you will!" she said staunchly.

Brenda faced Chris with a sheepish but grateful smile. "Thanks, Chris. I'm glad you feel that way. It gives me hope." She reached for a sponge, and the smile faded quickly from her face as she began wiping down the counter with strong, vigorous strokes. "I only wish Brad felt the same way."

"Brad?"

"Yeah, Brad." Brenda sniffed in annoyance. "Today he acted as if I had already failed, and I got the feeling he was ashamed of me."

"Brenda!" Chris exclaimed. "What are you talking about? Brad didn't say anything to make you think that."

Brenda wheeled around. "I didn't say he *said* anything, Chris. It's what he didn't say." Brenda's voice trembled. She took in a deep breath and stared down at the sponge in her hand. With the other hand she swept her hair out of her eyes and looked at her sister, a hurt expression on her beautiful face. "Everyone else — *everyone* — took my side, Chris." Brenda almost added, "Even you," but cut herself off. Chris's sincere support came as a welcome surprise. "But not Brad. He didn't say anything about maybe McQuarrie was being unfair, maybe it wouldn't be so hard to pull up my grade." Brenda tossed the sponge into the sink and paced over to the refrigerator. She toyed with the bright strawberry magnet holding down the week's shopping list. When she continued, her voice was strained. "Brad just stood there, staring at me like he was embarrassed to know me. Imagine. Brad Davidson's girl friend not graduating high school. How humiliating. That's what he was thinking. It was written all over his face." Brenda stopped suddenly and forced back the tears welling up in her eyes. She turned away from Chris and began noisily rearranging the little jars on the spice rack.

Chris was silent for a long time. Finally she said quietly, "You're overreacting, Brenda. I don't think Brad was thinking anything like that. You're jumping to conclusions, and it's not very fair of you."

Brenda spun around and faced her sister. "Well, then, why didn't he say anything?"

Chris shrugged and looked pensive. "I don't know," she said slowly. "Brad's kind of straitlaced. It probably is hard for him to imagine failing. But I'm sure he's not embarrassed by you. He loves you, Brenda. You know that."

*Does he?* Brenda wondered silently, then shook her head to rid herself of the scary thought that maybe he no longer did. Maybe at Princeton he'd gotten used to more high-powered girls, more driven and directed. More like himself.

Chris sat down on a stool at the counter and spun around on it thoughtfully. "Brenda, you've got to give Brad a chance. At least talk to him tonight. Ask him why he didn't stick up for you. I'm sure he didn't mean to come across that way. Give him a chance to tell you so himself." After a pause, she added gently, "Sometimes you do tend to jump to conclusions, you know."

Chris's reserve made Brenda chuckle. "I can't argue with that, Chris." Brenda glanced at the clock and put a nervous hand to her hair. "My hair's a mess. If Brad sees me like this, I might scare him off for good. Then I'd never get a chance to find out what he really thinks of graduation and chemistry and his girl friend possibly failing!" With that she hurried up to her room. She had barely finished pulling on her new white pants and striped T-shirt when the doorbell rang.

"It's Brad," Chris called up, as cheerful and casual as if the conversation in the kitchen had never taken place.

Brenda checked her reflection in the mirror one last time. Her large dark eyes looked a little worried, and she seemed a bit pale. She brushed some blush on her high cheekbones and put a touch more gloss on her full lips. She had looked better, but considering how her stomach was churning, she decided she looked pretty good. She hurried along the upstairs hall and paused at the head of the stairs to catch her breath. She quickly reviewed in her mind exactly how she'd talk to Brad in the car on the way to Garfield, how she'd ask him about his feelings this afternoon. Brenda tried to pull herself together, then she bolted down the steps right into Brad's arms.

"Well, hi, there!" he said, as if absolutely nothing had gone wrong between them.

Brenda lifted her face toward his, and the look Brad gave her melted away all her fears. "They aren't home," she whispered in answer to his unasked question.

A soft smile played around Brad's lips as he pulled Brenda down off the last step. His hands smoothed over the silky skin of her neck and found their way up to her hair. He bent over her and gave her a long, gentle kiss that Brenda wished would last forever.

"If only we could stay just like this," Brenda murmured, not really meaning to say the words aloud.

"I know what you mean," Brad said huskily, then slowly pulled himself away.

"But Garfield's calling," Brenda said with a wistful sigh. She kept hold of Brad's hand and started for the door.

"Uh, I was thinking. Maybe you could skip it tonight."

Brenda arched her right eyebrow and waved a finger in Brad's face. "Duty calls," she said throatily, reaching up to brush his cheek with her lips.

Brad laughed uncomfortably. "That's not what I meant."

Brenda tilted her head and regarded him with puzzled eyes.

He let go of her hand and walked back toward the hall table. Beneath his black folding umbrella was a thick book. Brenda read the spine: *General Chemistry*.

Brenda wrinkled her nose. "Should I borrow that? We used a different book this year." She still didn't understand what Brad was up to.

"Uh, no." Brad shifted from foot to foot. He stuffed his hands in his pockets and leaned back against the front door. "Actually, I was going to suggest we study together tonight. In fact I — "

"Brad," Brenda said patiently. "I can't tonight. Not until later. Then I'll have to study alone. I've got to see Kara tonight, Kara Wakely, the girl I told you about. She ran away from home again yesterday. Fortunately she turned up at

Garfield. I've got to be there for her tonight."
Brenda reached past Brad for the doorknob.

"But I made up a study schedule for you," Brad
said, not moving.

"We can talk about it in the car."

"Listen, Brenda." Brad took both her hands in
his and led her to the stairs. He pulled her down
beside him. Brenda resisted only slightly. She
glanced at the clock. They still had a few minutes
before they absolutely had to leave. "Chemistry
in itself is no big deal. It's too bad it's a Kennedy
requirement, but it is. You *have* to graduate.
That's the most important thing you have to do
right now — more important than going to Garfield. You should skip it tonight."

"Skip it?" Brenda pulled her hands out of
Brad's and looked at him, incredulous. "I can't
let Kara down now. She needs my help. Besides,
I'm leading Tony's rap group tonight. He won't
be there. In fact, that's what I wanted to talk to
you about — " Before she could tell Brad about
the job Tony had offered her, he interrupted.

"Don't you understand, Brenda?" Now Brad
was beginning to sound exasperated. He jumped
off the steps and stood looking down at her.
"You're the one who's about to fail high school.
*You're* the one who might not get the diploma.
*You* need help now."

"What are you talking about?" Brenda's voice
rose slightly. She eyed Brad suspiciously. "Are
you trying to tell me that counseling at Garfield
isn't important?" She got to her feet and walked
to the far side of the foyer, wanting to put some

43

distance between them. "How can you imply that, Brad? You know helping other people is the most important thing in my life right now! I can't just drop Garfield as if it's . . ." — Brenda searched for the right word — ". . . some kind of hobby, some kind of after-school activity."

"I didn't say that," Brad said tensely. "I just said that at the moment you have to think about yourself, *your* future, first. Not Carol's or Kara's or whatever her name is."

Brenda couldn't believe her ears. Of all people, Brad should understand about Garfield. All along he had supported her work at the halfway house, even when her parents and Chris were skeptical. "Listen, Brad, we can talk about this in the car. I am committed to going to Garfield tonight. If you won't drive me, I'll catch the bus. But I can't be late."

Brenda marched to the door with Brad close at her heels. He grabbed his book and umbrella from the table and hurried behind her down the walk. Without saying a word, he opened the door of the car. Brenda hesitated only a minute before climbing in.

She waited until they were out of the driveway to speak. When she turned to Brad, her eyes were accusing. "Brad, I don't know exactly what's going on with you tonight, but maybe it's about time you were up-front with me. I don't know what you're trying to prove by telling me that helping people at Garfield House comes second right now. Why don't you just come out with the truth: You're so upset about the prospect of your girl friend not passing a dumb final, and possibly not graduating, that you're embarrassed."

"I'm *what*?" Brad sputtered, incredulous. "That's not true, Brenda. You have no right to say that. I'm just trying to help you."

"Well, you're the only person who didn't stick up for me today."

"What did you expect me to do?" Brad asked angrily.

"Take my side, like everyone else did. At least tell me you knew I could do it. At school you looked at me like I was someone you didn't want to know." Brenda struggled to keep her voice steady. For a few minutes she had actually believed Brad's reaction in school had been all in her mind. But now she could see that wasn't true.

Brad was silent for the rest of the drive. He pulled up in front of the old Georgetown brownstone that had been transformed into the halfway house and turned to Brenda with a hurt, confused look on his face. "You're wrong, Brenda, I don't know how you could accuse me of being embarrassed by you. I just want to help you. If I didn't think you could pass, I wouldn't try to help you. I don't know what I have to do to make you believe that."

Brenda met his glance head-on. All at once she wasn't sure if Brad was right and she was wrong. Had she been overreacting? Did studying for this test mean having to give up even her time at Garfield? Every instinct inside her said no. But even in her heart of hearts she didn't have a clue as to whether or not she could believe that Brad wasn't embarrassed, that he really did want to help her for her sake, not his.

"Listen, I can't talk about this now. I'm late," she said, gathering her bag.

"I'll pick you up later," Brad said. It was their usual arrangement. Brad would pick her up, and then they'd go to Mario's or to the movies. But tonight it didn't sound like a good idea to Brenda.

She climbed out of the car and paused with her back to Brad. She shook her head no, then said, "I'll get a ride home with Matt and Pamela. The meeting will run late." Without saying good-bye, she slammed the car door and hurried up the steps.

# Chapter
# 5

The overhead fan spun lazily, spilling weird shadows onto the rec room's cracked linoleum tiles. Thunder rumbled in the distance and a fitful hot breeze blew through the open doors and windows of Garfield's ground floor. Most of the halfway house residents were up in their rooms or hanging around out in the living room watching the Orioles play the Red Sox.

The staff planning meeting was going terribly, and Brenda felt as though it were all her fault. She had walked into the halfway house in a lousy mood, and she hadn't bothered to get out of it. The rap session earlier had been far from successful, and now, just when Tony was looking to Brenda for help, she was letting him down. She felt guilty, but she just didn't have the energy to get out of the dumps. If she hadn't had to wait for Pamela and Matt to drive her home, she would have left, pleading a headache. She wouldn't have been lying, either. Since her argument with Brad, she'd had this dull, heavy feeling right behind her eyes, making it hard to think, to talk, to concentrate on anything.

She could feel Tony's eyes on her as she stared down at the floor, tracing a path across the cracked linoleum with the nail of one finger. But she didn't look up. She didn't want to meet Tony's eyes. He'd ask her what was wrong, and she wouldn't know how to answer.

After a long silence, Tony finally cleared his throat. "What we need is some inspiration," he said to the little group gathered around him on the floor. "Matt brought up a good point earlier this evening. Several of the kids here are going to graduate from high school this month. Given the trouble they've had getting through the past year or so, graduation is really something to celebrate. But how to celebrate here at Garfield and make the party something special is the question. Any ideas?"

Matt Jacobs leaned his elbows back against the seat of the lumpy old couch and stretched his legs out in front of him. "Well," he said slowly, his deep, gravelly voice echoing in the sparsely furnished room, "I was thinking that maybe that art show of Garfield residents' work Pam was thinking of putting together might come in handy now. We could have an opening for that — make it a regular big party and honor the graduates."

"I don't know about that," Pamela Green said in a soft voice. "None of the kids graduating have taken my art course. Why would the show be special for them?" Like Matt, Pamela was a Kennedy junior Brenda had recently recruited to work as a volunteer at Garfield. While Matt taught a hands-on course in auto mechanics, Pamela ran an art workshop, one of Garfield's most popular programs.

"Pam's got a point," Tony admitted. "Still, I think the end-of-year art show could coincide nicely with whatever graduation party we give. We could put the show up, have an open house for that, but throw a separate party — say, the same night — for the graduating seniors."

"And keep it just for the Garfield kids," Matt added. "After all, we're like a big family here. We can schedule it before graduation day so no one's real family will get upset if the kids come here to celebrate."

"Good point, Matt," Tony approved. "So, I guess that's that for tonight. Let's talk again next week about food and decorations, and then we can set a date. Until then, let's keep a lid on this. I've got half a mind to make this a surprise party."

Matt and Pamela readily assented. Brenda wasn't listening. Her ears were tuned to the sound of rain pelting the sidewalk outside. The idea of kids at Garfield graduating when she might not made her feel pretty bad. Feeling bad — jealous, even — made her feel guilty in turn. What was the matter with her? Helping these kids get back on their feet, giving them a chance like Tony had once given her, had been the most important part of her life the past year or so. Did facing some problems of her own again mean she didn't have time or sympathy left to help others? Was everything she had said to Brad about the importance of working with other people a lie?

As Tony stood up and stretched his muscled arms high above his head, Brenda felt his eyes studying her. She scrambled to her feet. "Hey, Matt," she called, racing after the couple leaving the room. "Don't forget, I need a ride home."

"Brenda!" Tony called her name.

She stopped at the door and hesitated before turning around. "Yeah?"

"Want to talk?" Tony leaned back against the pool table, a cue stick in his hand. His eyes searched Brenda's, and the puzzled expression on his face gave way to a worried frown. "Something happened?"

Brenda didn't reply.

"With Brad?" he asked.

Brenda let out a deep breath and nodded. "Yeah, things got a little sticky tonight. But it's nothing I can't deal with."

Not taking his eyes off her, Tony rolled his shoulders and worked out a crick in his neck. "I can live with that," he said carefully. "But remember, other people here are counting on you now. Kara Wakely's in a pretty bad way. Don't let your own problems interfere."

Brenda dropped her gaze. Tony hadn't been at the rap session tonight, but he had obviously sensed Brenda couldn't possibly have been much help to Kara. Brenda vowed somehow to make it up to him. Right now she looked up at Tony, and said, "I won't, Tony. This is something I'd like to deal with alone. If I can't . . ." — she swallowed hard — ". . . well, I always have your number." She managed to crack a small smile.

50

"Now that's my favorite girl!" Tony's kind face lighted up with a wide grin. He strode across the room and gave Brenda a friendly hug. Brenda hugged him back, then turned and left the room before she changed her mind and poured out her heart.

Brenda was surprised when Matt walked out the door and deliberately bypassed his battered Camaro and steered her and Pam around the corner, down the street into the heart of Georgetown. "Where are we going?" Brenda sputtered, half running to keep up with Matt, wiping the rain from her eyes. It was really pouring now, and thunder and lightning cracked and flashed at frighteningly quick intervals. Pam hurried along beside her, pulling the collar of her paint-stained work shirt up around her neck.

"Next Wave Café," Matt said, turning another corner and opening a door leading to a bohemian-looking coffee house. Tiny diamond-shaped tables filled the small room, and bright expressionist prints decorated the pale stucco walls. Pam instantly walked up to the nearest canvas and studied it intently. "Hey, this is great!" she said, flashing Matt an appreciative smile.

The air conditioning was on full blast, and Brenda gave an involuntary shiver as she wrung the water from her hair. "I really have to get home," she said.

"*You* really have to talk!" Matt corrected her, as he firmly put his hands on her shoulders and sat her down next to Pam at the nearest table. He signaled for the waitress, but before she turned up he addressed Brenda in a firm, no-nonsense voice. "Tony wasn't there to see, but you really weren't there for Kara tonight."

Brenda flushed and started to protest that what happened at rap sessions was her business, not his. She was in charge when Tony wasn't around, not Matt Jacobs. Pam broke in before Brenda could say a word.

"Matt —" Pam cautioned him with a look, then turned to Brenda. "Listen, we're not here to dump on you. Nothing like that. It's just, we can tell you're really upset. It showed tonight. Everyone sensed it. It seemed wrong somehow for you to have a problem and not share it with the rest of the kids, with us. We're your friends, Brenda." Pam reached out a hand and squeezed Brenda's arm.

Brenda released a sigh and gave a little shudder. She pushed her hair back from her face. It was soaking wet and stuck in clumps to her head and the back of her neck. She reached for the hot chocolate that had miraculously appeared in front of her and cupped the warm mug gratefully in her cold hands. "Sorry, Matt. I deserved that," she said quietly. She picked up a spoon and poked a hole in the spiral of whipped cream, pushing it down into the frothy brew. "I wasn't honest tonight, and there was no excuse for that. I just was so embarrassed — I didn't know what to say. And then I had this fight with Brad." Brenda's thoughts suddenly seemed disconnected. Was she upset about not graduating, or Brad, or having to study, or what?

With great difficulty she related the day's events to her friends. Pam and Matt listened in silence

52

until she was finished. Then Brenda shook her head ruefully and said, "Once upon a time I used to be tough. Back then I would have said none of this matters. But it does now. I really care if I graduate along with the rest of my friends. I don't want to go to summer school. I want to stand up there and get my diploma in front of my family with the rest of the senior class. But I still can't believe how Brad has been treating me since he found out about this. He thought I should give up Garfield tonight and stay home and study. He just doesn't understand how important Garfield is to me." Brenda bit her lip and stared back down into her mug. "Of course," she said with a little shrug, "the way I acted tonight during the rap session and at our meeting, I wasn't a help to anyone. So, who am I kidding?"

"Stop being so hard on yourself," Matt said, gently tousling Brenda's tangled hair. "Everyone has off nights. You're usually so on, so up-front and honest at every session. Don't worry about whether you're right for counseling people. We already know that you are. Just being around you I've learned a lot these past few months."

"Me, too," Pamela said loyally. "And," she added after a moment's hesitation, "don't be so hard on Brad, either. I think he just wants to help you. But he looks at the world a bit differently than you do."

The earnest tone in Pam's voice made Brenda smile. "You can say that again." She gave a throaty laugh. "We're as different as night and day. Sometimes we do have communication problems. It's only natural, I guess," she said, won-

53

dering if maybe she had been making mountains out of molehills with Brad. Well, she'd give him a chance. As soon as she got home she'd call him and apologize.

"And you owe it to yourself to pass the test," Matt said reaching for the check. "No matter what you're feeling about Brad and McQuarrie, getting your diploma is more important. Don't forget, if you want to work as a counselor you've got to go to college sooner or later."

"I know," Brenda groaned, getting up. "I only hope that after this final I'll never have to look at a chemistry book again." Her face brightened considerably as she added, "And that's motivation enough to make me study hard enough to ace McQuarrie's final."

In the darkened upstairs bedroom, Brad Davidson lay on his bed with all his clothes on. He didn't have the energy to get undressed and crawl under the covers. His head was buzzing, and he knew there was no way he could sleep until he figured out what had happened tonight between him and Brenda.

He rolled over on his stomach and punched the pillow beneath the cotton spread a couple of times, then propped his chin in his hands and stared out the window over the wet streets of Rose Hill. If he craned his neck ever so slightly, he could just catch a glimpse of the streetlight at the end of the Austins' block. Looking that way now, he tried to picture what Brenda was doing. Maybe she wasn't even home from Garfield yet. Sometimes the rap sessions went on for hours, and she had mentioned something about a meeting afterward. If he were in her shoes, he'd be home already, burning the midnight oil studying.

He flopped back down on his back and tried to sort out his thoughts. He ran over every detail of his conversation with Brenda. Had it really been so unreasonable to remind her that though Garfield was a good thing, it wasn't her whole life; that come next year a whole new world would open up before her, and there were possibilities ahead she probably hadn't even dreamed of? That's what sometimes drove Brad crazy about Brenda: She tended to sell herself short. He agreed with her that she should be helping people, but Garfield was just a beginning. She had the makings of a really good psychologist—maybe a psychiatrist, if she could manage to push herself hard enough to get into med school.

But it wasn't the conversation with Brenda that rankled him. It was something else: this vague hazy feeling that somehow he was losing her. He'd had it ever since he'd gotten home from Princeton. He'd seen quite a bit of Brenda over the school year, at Christmas, over spring vacation, a couple of weekends here and there. Nothing had seemed wrong between them. If anything, Brad had felt closer to her.

Then, why now? He sprang to his feet and ran his hand through his thick straight hair as he walked to the window. Leaning his forehead against the steamy glass, he tried to get a handle on his feelings. Seeing Brenda alone always felt great, but seeing her with the crowd at the sub shop, or hanging out with her at Garfield House, felt different from how it used to. Something was different. No, not *something*. Brenda. Brenda was different. He had no idea why, but she just wasn't as close to him as she used to be, and he didn't know what to do about it. He wanted to ask her what was going on, but whenever they were together, the awful sensation that they were drifting apart seemed to vanish, and then it seemed pointless to discuss it.

Brad stared out at the rain and listened to the wind rustle the leaves of the tall oak outside his window. The phone rang twice before the sound registered, then his reaction was quick. His parents were sleeping. It was almost midnight. The call had to be for him.

"Hello?"

"Brad." Brenda's voice was hesitant. "Did I wake you up?" She was whispering. Brad's worried face softened into a tender smile.

"Oh, Brenda, I'm so sorry." He raked his hand through his hair and paced back and forth in front of his desk. "What happened tonight? I feel so mixed up," he said with feeling.

"*You're* sorry!" Brenda exclaimed with an air of self-disgust. "I'm the one who should apologize to you. I just overreacted, I guess. I was so upset about McQuarrie and all that. I went a little crazy."

It sounded to Brad like she was on the verge of tears. He wanted to rush out in the rain and run the half mile to her house. "Can you come out?" he asked very softly.

Brenda's low, throaty laugh was music to his ears. "Are you crazy? Past twelve on a school night? Daddy Austin would have me drawn and quartered." Brenda paused, then added a bit breathlessly, "But I would if I could; you know that."

"Yeah," Brad whispered. "You know — I love you."

"I love you, too." Brenda's voice was almost a sigh. Brad half expected her to hang up. But after a second she asked in a more normal tone, "Listen, does that offer of yours still stand?"

"You mean Mr. Davidson's private study hall?"

"Uh-huh."

"Tomorrow?" Brad asked.

"No way." Brenda moaned. "Remember, tomorrow night's your big night — and Chris's."

Brad laughed out loud, then, glancing toward the bedroom door, lowered his voice. "The Mayor's Youth Council dinner! Well, at least we'll see each other there."

"But we will set up a study date soon, okay? And meanwhile, I'll start hitting the books on my own. You're going to be surprised when you try to quiz me."

"I can't wait. I love your surprises," Brad said.

With great reluctance Brenda said, "Well, I guess it's good-night."

"Good-night, Brenda. Sweet dreams," Brad added. He hung up the phone and muttered to himself, "Davidson, you're stark raving mad. There's nothing wrong between you and Brenda. Absolutely nothing." A few minutes later he crawled into bed and immediately fell asleep with a huge, contented smile spread across his face.

# Chapter
# 6

"HELLO OUT THERE, CARDINALS! This is Karen Davis with your Friday wrap-up edition of *Newsnotes*. The big scoop, of course, is today is Senior Yearbook Day. That's right, folks — this year's long-awaited *Camelot* is hot off the press. The bad news is most of us juniors and underclassmen — except those hardworking *Camelot* staffers — don't get ours until Monday. And this edition is rumored to be the most exciting ever. I, for one, can't wait to get my hot littie hands on it!"

"Ditto to that, Karen. To celebrate this momentous occasion I've written a composition for synthesizer, book, and T square, in the style of John Cage. It's dedicated to this year's graduating class. I call it *Brian Pierson's Eclectic — Sixth Movement*."

The high-powered sound system Jeremy Stone and Bill Magnuson had hooked up on top of the photo file was turned on full blast, but Brian's eerie succession of page rustling, slippery sounds, and rhythmic taps was barely audible over the commotion in the cramped *Camelot* office. Chris Austin hugged her yearbook to her chest and stood in the middle of the room, feeling like the eye in the center of a storm. In small groups or pairs, seniors filed through the narrow, glass-windowed door to pick up their books from the cartons stacked in a corner. Minutes later they left laughing, shrieking, hugging one another, and jumping up and down. Chris herself couldn't keep the smile off her usually reserved face. She hopped from foot to foot in excitement as she surveyed the milling crowd.

By the water cooler, Ted and Bart were teasing Phoebe, tossing her yearbook back and forth above her head, not letting her read whatever they had signed in it. Phoebe's high, thick pony-tail was coming undone, and she was trying very hard to look annoyed at the boys, though her huge eyes were sparkling and a smile tugged at the corners of her mouth. "Why don't you just tackle them, Pheeb," Chris cried across the room. "Yeah, show those guys a thing or two," Kim Barrie's merry voice chimed in. Phoebe squinted and tried to look mean. To Ted's surprise, she flung herself directly at him, knocking the wind out of him and retrieving her book in the process.

Chris was still laughing when Janie Barstow walked up and gave her a hug. "Your picture looks great!"

Janie beamed, pointing over to the far wall.

Chris cringed slightly. She found the nearly

life-size blowup of her in her tennis whites highly embarrassing. Jeremy Stone had selected four of his favorite yearbook shots and printed them in his darkroom. Chris's photo was flanked by one of Woody, all smiles, bushy eyebrows, and suspenders; Phoebe in her worn-out overalls jumping over a puddle, her red hair flying in all directions; and an extraordinary, candid shot of Peter at the WKND control panel, his eyes squeezed shut, listening intently to music pouring into the earphones on his head. Looking at the pictures, Chris experienced a momentary pang of nostalgia. The depth of the feeling embarrassed her, and to cover her confusion, she started to laugh. She reached for Janie's book and started to sign it beneath the clear-eyed, crisp-looking photo of herself. While Janie signed her book, Chris leaned back against the drafting table and said, "Wow, it really is hard to believe it's all over." Her voice held no regret in it, just surprise.

"And it's becoming past tense faster and faster," yearbook editor Cynthia Walker chimed in, handing around a tray of Kim's homemade brownies.

"Yup. Pretty soon it will be finals week and after finals week there's graduation and after graduation — LIFE BEGINS," Peter Lacey's sonorous voice boomed through the office, and everyone in the room started cheering. Peter dropped his voice to a conspiratorial whisper and said to Chris, "I love working a crowd." He poked his face over Cynthia's shoulder and popped a brownie into his mouth. "By the way, great job,

Cyn!" Peter mumbled as he chewed and pointed to a copy of the yearbook with his elbow.

Cynthia flashed him a grateful smile and said simply, "It did come out nicely, didn't it."

Chris shook her head and ran her fingers appreciatively over the red embossed cover. "*Nice* isn't the word for it. I've never seen such a wonderful yearbook."

"I had a great staff," the editor said, wanting to give credit where credit was due. "Jeremy's wild layout ideas gave the *Camelot* a new look, and Laurie raised so much money that there's actually some left in the kitty for next year."

"Next year — where will we all be next year?" Peter mused, hoisting himself onto a desk.

"I heard you're going to UCLA," Bill Magnuson commented, walking up and slinging one arm around Cynthia.

Kennedy's ace DJ beamed with pleasure. "I can't wait, man. I really can't wait. The LA music scene is fantastic, and I'm going to be smack in the middle of it. How about you two?"

"Chapel Hill," the couple answered in unison, before Cynthia's attention was claimed by another conversation.

Chris regarded them with some curiosity. Bill and Cynthia were the only couple she knew outside of Henry and Janie who actually had landed in the same college. She felt a little envious. Even if Greg weren't just going into junior year next fall, there was no way they'd end up at the same college, because Chris had chosen an all-women school. Besides, after high school her boyfriend

61

planned to spend at least a year sailing around the world before settling down to college.

"Hey, Chris. What's up?" Brenda's throaty voice broke into her reverie.

"Hey, Bren. I haven't seen you all day. How'd things go with you and Brad last night?"

"Okay," Brenda said in a low voice. "Things got a bit worse before they got better. But it's more than better now."

Chris smiled knowingly. "I had a hunch about that. Especially when I was jogging this morning and saw a certain Ivy Leaguer, dressed for work on the road crew, picking up a certain senior at the Austin household at the most indecent hour of six-thirty A.M. to drive her to school!"

Brenda laughed and looked down at her feet. Her hair fell forward and covered her blushing face. "We just went to Dunkin' Donuts for breakfast. And for the first time in four years I wasn't late for homeroom," she added wryly.

"Speaking of homeroom, I had a message to deliver to Michael Rifkin during homeroom, and he never turned up. In fact," Chris looked around the room, "I haven't seen Michael all day. Hard to believe he wouldn't turn up to get his yearbook. Probably something came up with his music. Phoebe mentioned he was auditioning for Wolf Trap. Maybe she knows where — " Chris's voice trailed off, and her forehead creased into a frown. She had just spotted Phoebe by the door. Not ten minutes before, Phoebe had been horsing around with the guys and giggling over her yearbook. Now she looked as miserable as Chris had ever seen her.

Brenda followed Chris's gaze. "What's with Phoebe?" she asked, concerned. "A few minutes ago she was goofing around signing yearbooks as if she were Cyndi Lauper at an autographing session."

Chris didn't quite know how to answer her sister. For days now, Phoebe had been alternately happy, then down in the dumps. Chris felt a twinge of guilt. Phoebe had tried to confide in her about her fears of leaving school and her friends. But Chris had been too up and excited and caught up in the whirlwind of senior activities to really listen. Now she let out a thoughtful sigh and said, "I don't really know. Phoebe's been acting weird lately."

"Problems with Michael?" Brenda asked in a hushed voice.

With a firm shake of her head, Chris said, "No. She keeps getting the blues about graduating — " Catching Brenda's amazed expression, Chris giggled and tucked her shirt neatly into the waistband of her khaki skirt. "Would you believe it?"

Brenda twirled the long turquoise earring she always wore in her left ear and laughed sheepishly. "Can't say I feel the same — if I ever do get to graduate, that is," she added with a nervous laugh. "But it is a big step leaving high school, heading off to college. Phoebe's had some very happy moments here."

"Well, she looks anything but happy now!" Chris said, suddenly determined to get to the bottom of Phoebe's problem. Phoebe was drifting around the edge of the crowd, looking on the verge of tears. Chris could tell she needed someone to talk to. This time Chris was determined to listen, really listen to whatever Phoebe had to say. Without another word to Brenda, she started across the packed room to Phobe's side. But before she could get there, Phoebe slipped out the door and was gone.

Phoebe dangled her foot over the edge of the hammock, kicking at Shawn's skateboard with her bare toe and trying to figure out why her life felt like a terminal case of fill-in-the-blanks. Everyone she knew had their future neatly mapped out for them. Of course, she had a future mapped out, too: After school, vacation, after vacation four more years of school, after that, well, there's where the picture started getting fuzzy. Unlike everyone she knew, Phoebe still wasn't sure who she was or what she wanted to do.

The lawn sprinkler whooshed and whirred on the other side of the backyard, and though it was late afternoon, the sun still beat fiercely on her face and shoulders. Phoebe knew she should move into the shade or she'd end up with a sunburn she was really going to regret. But she didn't feel like moving; she almost felt she had earned the right to be as miserable as she wanted. After all, hadn't the yearbook staff dubbed her "Most Likely to Be the Happiest Girl in the World"? She glanced back down at the book in her lap, wistfully traced the delicate gilded design of a castle on its cover with her finger.

*"Camelot!"* she murmured. Four years ago when she got her first copy of the Kennedy High yearbook, she had wondered at the name. What

did King Arthur's court have to do with the sleek, modern high school in a D.C. suburb? Sasha hadn't been sure, either, and they had looked up the word *Camelot* in the dictionary: "a time, place, or atmosphere of idyllic happiness." And that for the most part, was what Kennedy had been for Phoebe until now. There'd been some tough times, some ups and downs, but looking back, she realized she had loved being in high school. Chris, Sasha, Woody, Michael — she loved all her friends, and she was afraid she'd never meet such great people again anywhere. That's why Peter's remark this afternoon in the yearbook office about real life about to begin at last had shot through Phoebe's happy mood like a bullet. These had been the happiest four years of her life, and now all the kids she knew were acting as if high school didn't matter at all, as if it wasn't even "real"!

Why was everyone so eager to move on? And why was she so afraid of it? Phoebe sat up and hung her legs over the side of the hammock, swinging them back and forth. Again she looked down at the yearbook, this time opening it and slowly, carefully, turning the pages the same way she had earlier that afternoon. Pictures of teachers and staff, none of them signed yet, gave way to shots of the underclassmen. Already half the juniors she knew had scrawled corny messages in the margins of the pages. When she got to the head shots of the seniors, she slowed down.

Chris's photo was stiff, not doing justice to her All-American good looks. But Phoebe didn't really look at the photo. She read Chris's prediction aloud. It was no surprise: "Most Likely to Be First Woman President." She thumbed ahead a few pages. Bart Einerson grinned up at her, looking like the handsome hero of a spaghetti Western. He'd only been at Kennedy since September, but choosing a "Most Likely to . . ." for him must have been a cinch: "Cattle Baron." He made no secret of wanting to run his family's prosperous Montana ranch. Sasha was, of course, "Most Likely to Win the Pulitzer Prize and Become Our Country's First Woman Poet Laureate." Woody was assured a future in the circus after his jokes blew a fuse in the Great White Way. And Michael — Phoebe sighed deeply, reading the caption under his picture. She was so proud of him. The yearbook staff had named him the next Zubin Mehta, though secretly she thought he'd end up being the cellist in a very great string quartet.

Phoebe closed the book in her lap and leaned forward, pressing her forehead hard against her knees. She didn't have to read her own prediction again. She had read it the minute she got home and had wanted to scream. She didn't want to be the happiest person in the world. She didn't want to be the kind of person that everyone seemed to think she was: lovable, warm, and sweet. Even Chris, her very best friend, had signed some corny message about her sweetness. By the time Phoebe finished reading half of what her friends had written in her yearbook, she felt like some sort of sugar-coated candy, and she hated the feeling. The only message she appreciated was Shawn's. On his way to the Little League game, he had scrawled a particularly vile version of an old rhyme inside the cover. Phoebe reread it now and grinned:

*Roses are red,*
*Violets and blue,*
*Lizards are slimy,*
*And so are you!*
    *Stay that way forever!*
        *Love, Shawn.*

Phoebe closed the book, feeling particularly grateful that the publication of *Camelot* had coincided with Shawn's current gross-out phase, and not with last year's endless barrage of dreadful knock-knock jokes.

"Phoebe!" Mrs. Hall stuck her head out the kitchen window and yelled across the yard. "Sasha's on the phone. She's calling from Laurie Bennington's and wants to know if you're coming to the meeting tonight."

"A meeting?" Phoebe repeated, then groaned. Tonight was the planning session for Woody's Roast. Phoebe checked her watch. She had to shower and wash her hair before Michael got back from Wolf Trap. "Uh, yes. Of course. Tell her I'll see her there, Mom. I'll be a little late. Michael won't be here until eight."

Phoebe sprang to her feet and hunted in the grass for her sandals. If only there were something she was really great at doing, there'd be no question about what she should do with her life. Like Michael. At the moment, Phoebe was a little jealous of her boyfriend. He never had to face these questions. He was born to be a musician. Phoebe was born to be — well, just Phoebe, it seemed. As she crossed the lawn, her soft face creased into a frown. Even though she could sing and act and did well in almost all her subjects, it was obvious that nothing about Phoebe Hall was outstanding enough to be mentioned in the yearbook. And as nice as being happy was, it seemed to Phoebe she didn't have any future at all.

# *Chapter 7*

Laurie's house was ablaze with light. Phoebe hoped Woody's Roast would turn out to be half as festive as the planning session for it. By the time she and Michael arrived, everyone involved in putting the party together was there, even Kim. Woody tended to stick to Kim like glue, and as Phoebe waved hello, she wondered exactly how Kim had disposed of Woody for the evening.

A loud argument was in full swing. Everyone seemed to be enjoying it, but Phoebe couldn't fathom exactly what the problem was. It seemed to have something to do with moving the Benningtons' long antique Swiss peasant dining table from the dining room to the rec room. The boys in the crowd were balking at the prospect of such hard work.

Michael instantly jumped into the fray. Phoebe hung off to the side, hoping mere exposure to all the commotion would get her more revved up for the wild party planned for one of her best friends. She plopped herself down in an empty corner of the deep-cushioned couch and tore a slice of pizza off the steaming pie nestled in a Mario's box on the coffee table.

"A roast is like a banquet!" Laurie pronounced archly as she passed some pretzels and soda in Michael's direction. "So we should set the table up like a dais!"

"Good grief, we're not crowning Webster king of anything!" Ted Mason groaned, reaching for a Coke.

His girl friend, Molly Ramirez, lay on the floor, her dark curly head in Ted's lap. She looked up with innocent blue eyes and gave a wicked little laugh. "But it's his night to stand center stage and get some verbal tomatoes thrown in his face. Raising the table up will make it more like a stage. Besides, Woody just *loves* to make a spectacle of himself."

"We should hold this roast in a restaurant," Dick Westergard declared, stretching his long legs across the plush carpet. "All we'd have to worry about is the program and the jokes. This is beginning to sound like too much work."

"What's wrong with holding it here?" Laurie snapped at her boyfriend.

"Nothing. Nothing at all," Janie soothed and flashed Dick a warning look. "Besides, it's too expensive to have just our crowd rent a place for the night."

"Of course, if someone intends to foot the bill, it would save me a lot of trouble," Laurie pouted, obviously hurt that her friends didn't think her elaborate house was suitable for the occasion.

"Your house is perfect, just perfect," Michael spoke up and ruffled Laurie's shiny hair. Unused to such spontaneous affection from one of the crowd, Laurie pulled back a little, embarrassed, but obviously pleased.

"But it'll be more fun here, anyway — and maybe, just maybe, we can use the pool," Monica Ford added warmly.

"Can Woody swim?" a wide-eyed Fiona Stone asked.

"He's so full of hot air, he floats!" Bart howled.

"No dunking Woody until after the videos!" Jeremy warned nervously. "I don't want all that equipment I'm borrowing from the media department to get wet."

"Now, about those videos . . ." Jonathan began.

Phoebe tuned out the rest of the discussion. Pleasant as planning Woody's party was, she just wasn't in the mood to be of much help. Making an apologetic comment to no one in particular, she got up off the pale gray couch and drifted through the open French doors into the Benningtons' sprawling backyard. She knew eventually Michael would follow her, and she wondered why that thought didn't make her happier. Light spilled out of the living room onto the perfectly manicured lawn. Laurie's yard always reminded Phoebe of a golf course, and every time she came here, she had a terrible urge to sow a sackful of dandelion seeds on the spongy green sod. Suddenly she wondered if after graduation she'd be too grown-up to do that kind of thing.

Of course, she never really *had* played tricks or high-spirited practical jokes like some of her other friends had: Phoebe grinned remembering the time Ted and the rest of the football team had dumped a bucket of pink paint on the statue of Robert E. Lee outside Leesburg Academy. And just last week Molly and Katie Crawford had earned themselves immortality in the annals of Kennedy history when they dumped red dye in the swimming pool just before the boys' swim meet practice. Of course, Katie had almost lost her boyfriend, swim team captain Eric Shriver, and both girls got two weeks of detention. Phoebe had never gotten detention in her life. Face it. She was just too good. "Ms. Congeniality!" she groaned, always doing the right thing. She felt about as interesting as a piece of cotton candy.

Michael found her sitting by the side of the pool, tossing blades of grass into the dark water. He dropped down beside her, his shoulder just brushing hers.

"Nice out here, isn't it?" he said. His musical voice sounded like a song.

When Phoebe didn't answer, Michael cleared his throat and asked tentatively, "Is something wrong, Pheeb? You seemed a little put off or something when I turned up."

"No, Michael," Phoebe answered instantly and reached for his hand. "Nothing's wrong with us, at any rate." She knew that was the truth, even though seeing Michael's van pull up in her driveway earlier hadn't made her happy at all. Phoebe wondered why.

At her declaration, Michael's body relaxed. He reached over to stroke Phoebe's hair, but pulled his hand back. Something about Phoebe said hands off. Something was definitely wrong. "So, what are you upset about, then?" he asked, allowing Phoebe to move away a little.

She tucked her hands in the pockets of her striped baseball knickers and said very slowly, "I think everyone makes too big a deal out of all this graduation stuff." Saying it aloud, she knew all at once that wasn't really what was wrong.

Michael pulled back slightly, a surprised look on his face. "Aren't you excited by it?"

Phoebe just shrugged.

Michael stretched out on the grass and propped his head on Phoebe's lap. "Well, I can't wait, myself. At last, all this will be over." He gazed up past Phoebe's loosely flowing hair at the stars.

Phoebe frowned. "That's what everyone seems to feel." Her tone implied "everyone" certainly didn't include her. "I mean, what's wrong with 'all this'?" Phoebe flung her arms open wide, embracing the warm night air.

Michael couldn't keep the smile off his face. He lifted his head, leaned on one elbow, and studied Phoebe. "Nothing; it's just fine. Except, in a few more weeks we have a chance to start our lives, for real — "

Phoebe broke in with a passion that surprised them both. "There *you* go now. First Peter this afternoon, now you." She jumped to her feet and chafed her sunburned arms with her hands. She walked a few steps away from Michael, then paced back again. She stood there looking down at him for a moment. "For you it's different. You were probably born with a violin under your chin and a piano in your crib!" Phoebe cried almost vehemently. "Your whole life you've known exactly what you want to be." She corrected herself. "No! More than that. *Everyone's* known what you want to be, what you *are*! Oh, Michael, don't you see?" Phoebe's voice trembled. "For people like you and Chris and Peter, and all our friends, it's so wonderful to say 'Now I start my real life.' But what's the real life of Phoebe Hall? It's supposed to start in two weeks, and it feels like some kind of hole I'm about to fall in."

Phoebe sounded so frightened that Michael reached for Phoebe's hand and pulled her down beside him. "Hey, what's this about? You're not falling into any holes — I'm not going to let you." He laughed. "You sound like you've been reading too much *Alice in Wonderland*!" He pretended to scold her. Gently he brushed the wild red curls off her face. He was surprised to find her cheeks were damp with tears.

"Phoebe, Phoebe," he murmured, as he pulled her closer. "You're who you are. The most wonderful girl in the world on the brink of a wonderful life. Can't you feel it? Everyone else knows that about you."

His voice was so deep with feeling, Phoebe trembled. She wrapped her arms around him, pressed her face against his chest. His worn cotton shirt was cool against her burning cheeks. She leaned for a moment into his soothing hands, wishing he could take all her fears away. She wanted to believe him. She really did, but how could she make him understand? No matter how wonderful everyone thought her future was, no one could tell her *what* it held for her or who she was.

She swallowed hard and sniffed back her tears. Crying couldn't make things better. She sat back on her heels and looked down at her lap. Slowly she shook her head back and forth. "I know this sounds dumb. But everyone's so happy about being grown-up — because that is what this means, isn't it?" She lifted her troubled eyes toward Michael's face.

He was smiling a tender but puzzled smile. Phoebe continued, hoping he wouldn't laugh at her. "But Michael, I don't know yet what I want to be when I grow up. And I feel so weird about that."

Michael didn't laugh. He looked confused. "But you've decided to major in music and theater."

"Yes, I have," Phoebe answered edgily. "But is that really me? Those are two things I can do pretty well: act and sing. The original song-and-dance girl at your service." Her voice sounded strained.

"I wouldn't put myself down if I were you," Michael said, a hint of impatience in his voice. "You're talented, and you're going to pursue what you're good at. Besides, you've got *four years* to decide what you want to do with your life. I don't see the problem, Phoebe. Really I don't."

"Because you're more than just good at what you do," Phoebe cried. "The yearbook committee dubbed you the next Zubin Mehta! And Chris, the First Woman President, and Sasha, Pulitzer Prize Winning Journalist/Poet Laureate." Phoebe knew she sounded ridiculous, even envious of her friends, but she was too worked up to care. "But me," she tapped her chest with her finger. "I'm Ms. Congeniality."

"That's not what they said." Michael tugged his hair in visible annoyance.

"Well, just about — 'The Happiest Person in the World' — UGH!!" Phoebe spat the words out.

Michael's mouth fell open. "You're upset about that."

"Yes," she asserted.

"I — I don't understand."

Phoebe could have told him that. No one understood. She drew up her legs and curled her chest over her legs, pillowing her cheek on her knees. Laughter from inside the house broke the sudden silence. Gradually Phoebe's pulse slowed down. She stole a glance at Michael. He was looking out over the grass, toward where the roses were blooming. She could sense the wheels turning in his brain, trying to find something to say, some way to help her, some way to understand. A wave of warmth rushed over her. Whatever this problem was, Michael couldn't help it. In fact, he just made it worse, along with the rest of her friends. And it wasn't their fault. "Michael," she said after a short hesitation. "I'm sorry. I didn't mean to lay this on you. And I — I'm glad they think you'll be Zubin Mehta. I think of you as a Pablo Casals myself," Phoebe tried to joke.

Michael looked at her and gave an embarrassed smile. "What would I do without my Pheeberooni fan club!" He reached out and tousled her hair.

Phoebe captured his long-fingered hand between hers and kissed it. "I love you, Michael. I really do."

Michael got down on the ground beside her and lowered his face toward hers. "Now, that's enough to make me the happiest person in the world, if you're willing to give up the title!"

To prove exactly how willing she was, Phoebe kissed him with her whole heart and soul.

The sounds of the party breaking up drifted out over the breeze. "We'd better get our act on the road," Phoebe whispered, nuzzling Michael's ear, then pulling away and straightening her tank top.

"Not yet!" he whispered, pulling her back toward him. "I came out here to tell you some good news."

"Oh, I thought that's what you were doing!" Phoebe quipped, jumping lightly to her feet. Her sunburned back stung when she stretched her arms over her head. She slung her arm lightly around Michael's waist as they headed to the house to fetch her bag.

"No. My news is — " Michael stopped walking and pulled Phoebe over to the privacy of the rose arbor. "I'm not going to Juilliard after all."

He looked so happy that Phoebe thought she was seeing wrong. Maybe she had sunstroke and not sunburn. "Not going to Juilliard! What happened?" she gasped.

Michael let out a buoyant laugh. "Something wonderful." He hooked his hands around Phoebe's waist and stared down into her eyes. "Something incredibly wonderful, especially for us."

Phoebe regarded him suspiciously. Maybe *he* had sunstroke.

"I'm going to the Boston Conservatory of Music."

"In Boston?" Phoebe asked and immediately felt very dumb.

"Just an hour from Smith College in Northampton!"

"You did that for me?" Phoebe got a funny scary feeling. "You can't do that, Michael. It's your whole life and — "

"Whoah — I didn't say I did it for you." Michael hesitated, waiting to see Phoebe's reaction. She relaxed slightly. He went on. "That cello teacher I told you about. The one who usually just teaches at the Vienna Conservatory. Well, he's coming to Boston under a three-year contract. And I'm going to study with him there. It's a dream come true — two dreams, really," he added a bit huskily as he bent his head over hers.

Phoebe let him kiss her, but her mind was reeling. Sure, it was great Michael would be so close. *If* she really did end up going to Smith. But this afternoon while washing her hair, she'd gotten another idea. She planned to see her guidance counselor early the next week and check out some programs at other places. Maybe after talking to the counselor and reading some more, she'd find out what she really wanted to do, what she was really suited for. And if that meant having to go somewhere else for college, maybe somewhere far away . . . Phoebe let her thoughts trail off. She'd cross that bridge when she came to it. But as Michael hugged her, she wondered what he would say if she changed her mind and landed in a college nowhere near Boston *or* Northampton.

# *Chapter*
# *8*

Brenda checked the wall clock over her desk: six-twenty. Still an hour to go before Brad showed up to join the family for the dinner honoring Chris and some other local teenagers at the Rose Hill Inn. For the occasion, Brenda had set her hair and was waiting for the electric curlers to cool off.

She lay facedown on her bed kicking her legs up behind her, one elbow on her chemistry book, the other on her notes, her eyes riveted to the open pages of her yearbook. Though she had joked self-consciously with Chris and the gang about her description as "The Girl with the Mile-Wide Shoulders Most Likely to Save the World" and had groaned at the song *Camelot*'s editors had picked as her theme — "We Are the World" — Brenda was secretly proud. She wanted people to trust her, to confide in her, and if saving the world was something her friends believed she could do — the very thought sent a chill up her spine. She was too practical to think she'd save the world, but just to help one person, the way she'd been helped. . . .

She flopped over on her back and stuffed a couple of pillows beneath her head. When she had first arrived at Kennedy as a sophomore, she had certainly been one of the most unhappy people she knew. She had hated her new life in Rose Hill: Her stepsister, Chris, had seemed like a prissy, stuck-up snob; Chris's crowd, all movers and doers on the Kennedy scene, seemed to look down on her like she was some kind of down-at-the-heels loser; her new stepfather, Jonathan Austin, had criticized her and everything about her constantly: her clothes, her schoolwork, even the few people she had called her real friends. Nothing about Brenda seemed good enough for the Austins, so eventually she left. Running away, of course, hadn't solved a thing, but it had landed her at Garfield House. Slowly, with Tony's help, everything had changed.

Brenda thoughtfully gnawed the inside of her lip. She had changed — or rather, her attitude had — all because of Garfield, really. She owed so much to that place. She had friends now — dear, good friends. She had a sister she loved more than almost anyone and an incredible guy who really loved her. Working with Tony at Garfield had helped her figure out who she was and what she wanted to be.

She rolled over on her side and glanced back down at her yearbook and smiled. So many people had signed it and wished her well and seemed to believe in her. She wondered how Brad would sign it — if he didn't think signing yearbooks was mere kid stuff, she thought with a laugh. Then the laugh died on her lips. Brad was encouraging about her passing her chem test, and he truly wanted to help her study. But he still didn't seem to realize how much working with other kids meant to Brenda, even though everyone else seemed to.

A soft tap on the door cut into Brenda's daydreams. "Bren, can I come in?"

Brenda sprang up from the bed and automatically hid the yearbook under her pillows. "Sure," she said, flinging open the door.

Chris wore a deep blue dress that matched her eyes perfectly. In her hand she held a bunch of ribbons. From the expression on her face, Brenda could tell she was confused.

"I hate to bother you," Chris said apologetically, "but what should I do with my hair?" When she realized Brenda wasn't dressed yet, her eyes widened and her head jutted forward. "What are you wearing?" Chris asked. "And you set your hair?" she gasped, amazed.

Brenda burst out laughing and gave her curlers a self-conscious little pat. "I have to wait for these to cool before I put my party clothes on," she said with a smile. "And I promise," she said, steering Chris into the room, "that I won't wear these." She tugged at the waistband of her faded black jeans. "As for *your* hair — " She stepped back and eyed her sister critically. Chris looked very pretty, her cheeks still pink from the shower and her blow-dried hair glistening in the sunlight that poured through the window. "How about leaving it down and pushing it back with something really nice," Brenda suggested, then snapped her fingers and said with a grin, "I have just the thing."

As her sister opened the stained-glass box she used to stash her jewelry, Chris eyed her skeptically, then gasped with pleasure when Brenda pressed a pair of blue cloisonné combs into her hand. "These are beautiful, Bren; where did you get them?"

"Pamela's teaching a jewelry course at Garfield. One of the kids I counsel gave them to me. I thought you'd like them."

Chris leaned toward the mirror to put in the combs. Brenda smiled at her reflection and nodded. "You look great!"

Chris in turn helped Brenda pull the rollers from her hair. "So, how are things going at Garfield? Is Kara Wakely doing any better?" Chris asked with genuine interest.

Brenda's face darkened. "No, worse. And I wasn't very much help to her this week. What with worrying about chemistry, graduation — and Brad," Brenda added, almost hesitantly.

"I thought you two had smoothed things out."

Brenda reached for her brush and considered her situation with Brad silently before replying. She moistened her lips and said slowly, "We have. I think we have. It's just I wish sometimes he understood how much Garfield means to me." Brenda looked up into Chris's eyes. "The way you do — the way most of my other friends do."

Chris tilted her head and regarded her sister

carefully. "What makes you think he doesn't?" The surprise was evident in her voice.

Brenda tossed her brush down on the bed and went to get her dress from the closet. "Oh, I don't know exactly," she said, pulling the gray shift over her head. "Just, things."

A round of applause greeted Mayor Farrell as he got up from the table to begin his speech. Taking advantage of the commotion, Brad leaned close to Brenda, whispering in her ear, "You're the most beautiful woman in this room!" He ran his finger along the low-cut back of her loosely flowing dress, and Brenda got chills all over.

No one had ever called her a woman before, and the word sounded wonderful, as if at last she had grown into the right to live her own life. She couldn't help but break into a smile, but she put her finger to her lips to silence Brad. The mayor was about to present Chris with an award for being Rose Hill's outstanding high school graduate of the year. Brenda leaned forward in her seat and looked around the crowded Rose Hill Inn.

Local dignitaries as well as a few familiar personages from the D.C. political scene filled the elegant, low-lighted dining room. Brenda recognized some of Chris's favorite teachers from school. Even Mr. Beman, the principal, was there, with his wife and son, whom Brad had gotten to know at Princeton. From across the table Chris caught Brenda's eye. "Wish me luck!" she mouthed at her sister. Brenda flashed her a victory sign and smiled in turn at Greg, who had joined them for the celebration supper. Greg was beaming at Chris, and Brenda almost envied how proud he looked. She glanced sideways at Brad. He was listening intently to the mayor. Beneath the table she reached for his hand. Brad gave her an answering squeeze, and Brenda relaxed in her seat and turned her attention to the podium.

"To honor this outstanding student," Mayor Farrell said, looking down the long table directly at Chris, "on behalf of the citizens of Rose Hill, the faculty and staff of Kennedy High, and the Rose Hill City Council, I would like to present Ms. Christine Austin with this year's Mayor's Youth Award." The room burst into applause. The mayor gestured in Chris's direction. She blushed but stood up very tall and walked confidently to the podium. She bent her head so the mayor could drape a silver medal with a dark blue ribbon around her neck. Then he shook her hand and handed her an envelope, which Brenda knew contained a sizable scholarship check.

At the end of Chris's brief, well-phrased acceptance speech, Brenda clapped her hands louder than anyone in the room. She was so proud of her sister. This kind of event suited her perfectly. Not only did she look beautiful, and perfectly groomed, but she was so confident, so at home in front of the public. Brenda discreetly wiped away a tear as Chris walked back to her seat, her eyes focused on Greg's proud face. She was so happy for Chris, and so sure, at that moment, that her sister really might be America's First Woman President. It might be the only yearbook prediction that would come true.

"And now . . ." Mayor Farrell's voice rang out across the room. Conversation quieted down as the mayor glanced in Brenda's direction. She sank back in her seat, wondering what was going on. "It seems last year's winner of the Mayor's Award is here this evening as a guest of the Austin family. I would like Mr. Brad Davidson to get up and take a bow. From what I've heard of his academic exploits at Princeton, I think our medal was just the harbinger of a multitude of awards and prizes this young man is going to win in what promises to be a very distinguished life."

Brenda gasped. "Brad, he wants you to get up!" She nudged his leg with her hand. Brad looked over at her and rose slowly to his feet. Again the applause was warm and loud. The mayor motioned Brad to the podium. Brad politely begged off, but after a moment headed toward the head of the banquet table and addressed the crowd.

"Thanks to the mayor here, and all my friends," he made an expansive gesture around the room, but his eyes rested lovingly on Brenda, "I have had a good first year at Princeton. The confidence you have all shown in me has helped a great deal. Especially when the going got rough. . . ."

Brenda couldn't believe how polished Brad sounded, how sure of himself. He hadn't even expected to give a speech, not like Chris, who had rehearsed every word of her acceptance speech for days now. Brenda looked from Brad to Chris to Brad again. A little frown tugged at her smiling lips. She hadn't noticed it before, but they were so alike. So different from her. Brenda leaned back and fiddled with the long silver earring dangling from her left ear. The mayor's prediction that Brad was going to have a life full of distinguished awards started rankling her. Not that she'd begrudge Brad that. She wanted him to win the Nobel Prize for medicine, if there were such a thing. But was she the kind of girl who belonged with a guy like that? Someone so directed?

As Brad made his closing remarks, Brenda watched him carefully. He looked as comfortable as Chris in front of the audience. He positively glowed in the public spotlight and yet, like Chris, seemed to stay his normal everyday self. To speak to a crowd, he didn't have to put on an act, become something he wasn't.

Brenda knew she'd fold up and die in terror if she ever had to give a speech. She was good at talking at a rap session, but she was best working one-on-one with people like her, who preferred quiet places and staying out of crowds. Why did Brad even bother with someone like her? She hadn't asked herself that in a long, long time. Not since the time they'd met on a crazy school ski outing and Brad had first become interested in her.

The thought no sooner crossed Brenda's mind than she got a funny cold feeling in the middle of her chest. What was she thinking? She and Brad belonged together. They loved each other. Wasn't that enough? Did they have to be like two peas in a pod for a relationship to work?

Suddenly everyone was applauding, and Brenda looked up guiltily. Brad was making his way back to his seat, shaking hands with old teachers en route, but his eyes were on Brenda. His face was exultant, and he obviously looked toward her to share his joy. Brenda managed a smile. She wanted to be there for him, to tell him how wonderful he'd just been. But at the moment all she could think of was how truly humiliated he would feel if she didn't manage to pass that exam, didn't graduate. She wouldn't just be failing high school, she'd be failing him.

"How was it?" Brad asked eagerly, dropping down by her side. He took her hand between both of his and chafed it. A worried note came into his voice. "Your hand is freezing."

"Uh, the air-conditioning," Brenda said, knowing the air-conditioning had nothing to do with how cold she felt or why she was shivering.

"Are you getting sick?" Brad whispered and put a gentle hand on her forehead.

Without thinking, Brenda pulled brusquely away. "You can't play doctor yet, you know," she said, a bit sharply.

Brad regarded her with some confusion. "Is something wrong?"

"No." Brenda balled up the linen napkin in her hand, then unrolled it, and began smoothing it out over her lap. "I mean — yes — " She looked up at him a little wild-eyed. "Brad — " she started, a catch in her voice. But she didn't know what to say, so she took his hand back and whispered "I love you" with a fierceness that frightened her.

Her declaration obviously surprised Brad. He laughed as though he were embarrassed and said "Me, too. But I didn't think my speech was that good." He tried to joke, but something in Brenda's face made him turn serious. "Did I say something wrong?"

Brenda looked down at her hands. "No. You didn't say anything wrong." She paused. "You *never* do," she added almost glumly.

"Knowing you, that's not a compliment," Brad observed. "Should I have made a blooper?"

Brenda tossed her hair off her face. "Of course not. I think you gave a fine speech. I was just thinking how I could never give a speech like that," she admitted ruefully.

Brad threw back his head and laughed. Several people looked over in the couple's direction and smiled. Brad grinned sheepishly and lowered his voice. "Brenda, you can do anything you set out to."

Brenda didn't quite believe that. And she wasn't sure Brad did anymore, either. Especially when he said a moment later, "And speaking about things you have to do, how about hitting the books tonight. We can work together in your kitchen," he suggested with a smile.

"You want to leave now?" she asked.

"Why not?" Brad replied, straightening his tie and buttoning his jacket.

"Because I thought you wanted to spend more time out with me tonight." Brenda knew she sounded like a disappointed little girl. She didn't mean to, she just was suddenly afraid she was wrong for Brad, and sooner or later he'd realize that. And then. . . .

"Brenda?" Brad was looking down at her, puzzled. "Shall we go?"

"Boy! A girl could get the impression you were trying to get rid of her. Calling it an evening at nine P.M." Brenda struggled to keep her tone light, but she sounded miserable.

"Don't be ridiculous," Brad said, ushering her out of the dining room.

"Well, I certainly hadn't thought we'd be heading home so early. I mean, we never do." Brenda trembled on the brink of tears.

Just outside the coat check, Brad pulled her toward him. "We don't have to rush right home," he whispered, nuzzling her ear. His lips caressed her cheek, her forehead, and finally found her mouth. Brenda's lips responded to his, but she felt as if some kind of curtain had suddenly fallen between them.

# Chapter
# 9

The next Tuesday after French class, Phoebe stood outside the counseling office, her nose pressed against a framed poster of Yosemite National Park. Granite peaks surrounded a mirror-like lake, and tall pines drifted upward into the purest blue sky. Phoebe clasped her hands together and decided she had never seen any place so beautiful in her life.

"Get any closer you're gonna fall in!"

Woody's cheery voice made Phoebe jump. Instantly she hid the stack of brochures she was holding behind her back.

"Uh, hi, Woody!" she said with an embarrassed laugh.

Woody wriggled his bushy eyebrows and waved his finger in Phoebe's blushing face. "Now, what exactly is going on here?" He tapped the poster forcefully and observed, "The lady blusheth too much. If I didn't know you better, I'd say you were pining away for a forest ranger living in them thar hills!"

"Pretty good, Webster!" she joked. "You aren't entirely off the mark!" she added, tightening her grip on the fliers she still held out of sight.

"Hey, kid, don't tell me you're two-timing Michael behind his back." Woody pretended to look shocked. "Remember, if you need a shoulder to cry on, 'I'll be there.'" He sang rather than said the last words. Lifting an imaginary microphone to his lips, he closed his eyes and broke into a gravelly rendition of a torch song.

Phoebe tucked the brochures into her bag before beginning to applaud. "Good show, Woodrow Wilson Webster."

Woody flopped over into a deep bow. A broad, brawny hand reached out and pulled him up by his suspenders. "You'd better straighten up, Webster!" Bart barked in the manner of a drill sergeant. His sister Diana was by his side.

"Yes, *sir!*" Woody fell into the role and saluted smartly before whipping the Stetson off Bart's head and plopping it rakishly on his own.

"Is auditioning in the halls another senior tradition I've got to endure next year?" the tall, pretty blonde asked with a smile, as Bart led the little group downstairs toward the cafeteria.

"I wasn't listening. I was singing farewell to these hallowed halls," Woody sniffed loudly. He slung one arm over Phoebe's shoulder and guided her toward the end of the cafeteria line which was snaking out into the hall. "I was serenading our usual Tuesday lunch: Incredible Inedible Chili."

Amid the laughter that followed Woody's declaration, Phoebe pulled free of his arm. "Uh, sorry, I can't join you folks for lunch. I've got some studying to do."

"Pheeb, we only have one week of school left. You're *still* studying?"

"Yes. That last week is full of finals, and I've got to get some work done now," Phoebe asserted, cutting out of line and hurrying toward the nearest door. She wasn't really planning to study right now, but she did have some homework of her own to do and only a few days to do it in. She burst out of the building onto the sun-drenched quad and ducked around the side of the building where none of the kids she knew usually hung out.

She made for a secluded bench, then pulled an apple and the brochures out of her bag. Her talk with Ms. Murdock this morning had really inspired her. Suddenly her future didn't seem so bleak. The guidance counselor had more or less convinced her she could be anything she wanted. More importantly, she didn't say all Phoebe was good for was being happy.

Phoebe opened one flier after another: "Your Future as a Veterinarian"; "Agribusiness and You"; "So You Want to Go to Law School"; "Be a Forest Ranger." Phoebe tossed the other fliers aside and absently took a bite from her apple. She hadn't thought of being a forest ranger before now, though she'd always loved nature shows on television and had really enjoyed her camping trip last summer to Great Smoky National Park . . . except for the bears. Phoebe bit her lip and read the brochure carefully. She certainly had all the right qualifications: she was healthy, strong, worked well with people, loved being outdoors. She ran her finger down the list of college majors the Park Service considered appropriate: forestry, ethology (Phoebe wasn't sure what that was) ecology, life sciences. She liked science and was okay at it, but majoring in it in college seemed pretty formidable. But forestry. Phoebe let the idea kick around in her brain. That sounded nice. Vistas of New England forests bathed in autumn colors passed before her eyes. She seemed to remember that Cornell had a forestry program that was very good, and Ithaca, New York, wouldn't be all that far from Michael. It wouldn't be like going to study ecology in Berkeley, California. She tilted back her head to soak up the warm rays of sun and realized she felt better than she had in weeks.

Later that afternoon Phoebe tiptoed into the media room where Ted Mason was holding court. The popular football captain sat in front of Jeremy's camcorder wearing his football jersey *and* his baseball knickers. In one hand he held a bat. In the other, his football helmet. Karen was obviously having a hard time keeping a straight face during her interview.

"One last question, Ted. And I want you to consider your answer carefully. What was your most memorable moment at Kennedy High, the moment you want all your friends to remember you by ten years from now when they replay their video of the living yearbook."

Jeremy trained the camera on Ted.

Ted leaned back in the chintz-upholstered easy

chair and crossed his long legs. Then he uncrossed them again and leaned forward, propping his arms on the handle of his bat. "Beating the socks off of Leesburg last week in the baseball playoffs."

The audience of friends started cheering, and Jeremy cut off the tape. "Hey, guys, pipe down. This is Ted's interview."

"That's all right." Ted jumped up and indulged in a long stretch. "I've said all I can think of saying." He smiled apologetically at Karen.

Karen laughed and congratulated Ted warmly on his performance. Checking her clipboard, she murmured, "Let's see. Who's next? Uh, Phoebe." Karen looked around. "Oh, good, you're here." She smiled, gesturing for Phoebe to join her in the front of the room.

Phoebe sat down on the old chair and straightened the suspenders of her overalls. "Where'd you get this chair from?" she asked Jeremy, shielding her eyes from the lights. "It's soooo lumpy. And the lights are too bright," she complained, then took a deep breath. Karen was obviously ready to begin, and Phoebe was eager to hear the questions. Jonathan fiddled with the light stands until the glare was out of Phoebe's eyes.

"Tell it to them, Pheeb," Michael called in a stage whisper from the audience.

Phoebe blew him a kiss and smiled for the camera. Karen's first few questions were predictable and fun to answer. Who was her favorite teacher? What was her favorite moment? What had she hated most about Kennedy? Chicken Chow Mein. Phoebe mugged a disgusted face, reducing the audience to hysterical laughter.

"Ten years from now, what do you picture yourself doing?" Karen asked. "Singing at the Met? Starring in *Cats*?"

"She's already got a head start on that one!" Woody piped up. Karen flashed him a warning look, but Woody ignored it. "She's singing 'Memories' at graduation."

"That's a secret!" Michael groaned from the corner, then flashed an apologetic grin at Jeremy, who had flicked off the camcorder in disgust.

Phoebe couldn't help but smile. A part deep down inside her was pleased that at least in the living yearbook she'd be remembered as a person who was talented enough for Karen to ask about the possibilities of a stage career, even though a stage career seemed so impractical now. As Jeremy turned on the camera again, she sat forward a little in her chair and looked Karen directly in the eye. A day earlier she wouldn't have known how to answer the question. Suddenly everything seemed so simple and settled. "Maybe I'll do something like that," she answered quietly. She clasped her hands tightly in her lap before continuing. "But I've been thinking lately about how the future is full of adventures. Chris put that idea in my head. And I feel like doing something a little more" — Phoebe made a vague expansive gesture with her arms — "I don't know, adventurous, with my life." She paused a moment and tried to picture herself in the role of a forest ranger. The media room was hot and close, but Phoebe could feel a cool mountain breeze blowing through her hair and her Park Service scarf snapping in the wind. A sunny smile crossed her face, and she concluded in a brisk voice, "I'm thinking of becoming a forest ranger."

"What!" Molly Ramirez guffawed from the audience. "*You*, a forest ranger?"

Soon everyone in the room was laughing. "Hey, Pheeb. I'm supposed to be the class clown. Not you. You're stealing my thunder," Woody complained loudly.

Again Jeremy stopped the camera. "Come along now. What's the matter with all of you? This is meant to be serious."

Phoebe jumped to her feet. "But I am serious," she declared, staring stonily at Molly. "Just because you're a lifeguard and have already worked for the Park Service for a couple of summers, you don't have a monopoly on being a forest ranger."

"Hey," Molly cried, her blue eyes wide with surprise, "I didn't mean anything like that. I just never thought you were interested in outdoor stuff that much. That's all."

"Well, I am," Phoebe said staunchly. She stood up very straight and informed the crowd of her plans with great dignity in her voice. "In fact, I'm going to school for forestry now. I found out today that Cornell has a very good program."

"You *what*?" Michael sprang to his feet. Before Phoebe could repeat her statement, Michael threw his hands up in the air and stated, "That's ridiculous."

Phoebe's bottom lip began to tremble. She willed herself not to start crying. "Why, if *I* want to be something like a forest ranger, is it suddenly ridiculous? Ask Molly. Lots of girls do things like that now. Besides, why can't I have dreams, too?

Why won't anyone take me seriously?" Phoebe's voice broke, and she ran from the room crying.

Karen looked from Jeremy to Michael. "Did I say something wrong?" she asked, nervously smoothing the crease in her linen pants.

Michael shook his head. "No way. Phoebe's got this problem about what she's going to do with her life, and I think it's getting a little out of hand." He stalked into the hall to find Phoebe.

She was standing at the far end of the corridor, her back toward him, her shoulders shaking. She leaned her forehead against the window as she cried. Michael watched her for a second from a distance.

"Phoebe, what's going on?" he said, sounding a little tired. He leaned back against the window frame, his arms folded across his chest, and waited for her tears to subside.

Phoebe struggled to regain control. She wiped her nose with the back of her hand and gratefully accepted the tissue Michael produced from somewhere. "I'm sorry," she mumbled, then blew her nose. "I'm just so tired of people not taking me seriously. I really was serious just now."

"About going to Cornell?" Michael sounded genuinely surprised. She met his eyes and tried to explain herself. "I would have told you last night — not about Cornell, I only decided that now — but that I wasn't sure what I wanted to do was music and theater. No one really does think of me as the next Bernadette Peters." Phoebe tried to joke but Michael didn't even crack a smile. He was looking pretty grim actually, and Phoebe hurried to reassure him. "I don't want to go to

Cornell to be away from you, Michael. But if that's where I can study what I want to, then I'll go there. The way you'd have stayed at Juilliard if that cellist hadn't turned up in Boston."

Michael didn't look reassured at all. "But you don't really want to be a forest ranger, Phoebe. I don't know — " Michael tugged at his hair and searched for the word. "It's all made up."

"What do you mean, made up?" Phoebe asked sharply. "Ms. Murdock thinks I can do it. She thinks I can do anything. She's a guidance counselor, and she gets paid to tell people what they're good at."

"Phoebe." Michael sighed her name and leaned closer to her. He propped his elbows on the window sill and looked out over the quad. Taking her hand, he said with great patience, "You're probably good at just about everything. But what do you really love?"

Phoebe dropped her eyes. She searched her heart for the answer, then looked up, very confused. "Everything. Really. Just everything."

Michael's face lighted up in a wide, joyous smile. "That's the point. No matter what you do in life you're going to love doing it. And people around you are going to love you. Loving people and being loved is what really matters."

Phoebe snatched her hand from his. "Is that supposed to make me feel better?" she gasped in disbelief. "I don't believe you said that. You, of all people, Michael. You are one of the most career-minded people I know. How would you feel if someone said to you, 'Loving people and being loved is what really matters.' What if no one thought of you as a musician? How would you feel then?" She faced him with fiery eyes.

"But I *am* a musician, and I'm happy to be one, too. And of course I want people to love me," Michael responded.

"Well, I'm upset about being the most lovable blah at Kennedy High. I can't stand it anymore. The minute I want to do something serious, everyone laughs at me."

"Phoebe, you're overreacting," Michael said, his voice growing impatient.

"In my shoes you'd be overreacting, too," Phoebe cried in response. Michael reached toward her, but she pulled away out of his reach. "Leave me alone. I just want to be alone right now. I have some big decisions to make," she said. "And obviously you're not the person I can count on to help me make them." With that she spun away from him and strode down the hall.

"Good," Michael called after her angrily. "Because I don't intend to be there to help you, either!" He punched the fist of one hand into the palm of the other and walked to the opposite door. He stepped outside and gulped down a couple of breaths of flower-scented air. He loved Phoebe; he loved her more than he had ever loved anyone. But at the moment he couldn't believe she hadn't even given being near him next year a second thought. The realization hurt him, and at least for a little while, he wouldn't mind not being the shoulder she needed to cry on.

# *Chapter*
# *10*

"Why should I be up front if she's not?" Kara Wakely challenged the after-school group, her gray eyes cold, accusing. "Brenda keeps sitting around acting like somebody's big sister, like she's above it all. If you're so much better than me, than the rest of us" — Kara waved her arms a bit wildly around the group gathered in Garfield's therapy room — "why do you bother to come here, anyway? I know who your family is. Your sister's student body president at school. I read all about her in the paper this morning, getting that dumb Mayor's Award. People like you don't belong here," she spat, finally addressing Brenda directly.

Brenda recoiled as though Kara had slapped her in the face. She stared in disbelief at the pale, skinny girl sitting across from her. Kara's eyes smoldered with hostiilty. She gave her frizzy brown hair an angry tug, then abruptly averted her glance from Brenda's. Before Brenda could gather her wits about her to come up with some kind of response, Tony intervened. Brenda was grateful just to hear the sane, steady tenor of his voice.

"Kara," he said evenly, "no one's accusing you of not being up front. You only have to share whatever you feel like sharing in this group. You don't have to say anything you're not ready to. That's not how we work here. Just remember you're dealing with Brenda in this session, not her family. Everyone here has a story, or they wouldn't be involved with Garfield."

Kara scowled at the group leader, then stared hard at a colorful painting on the wall.

Brenda barely had time to breathe a sigh of relief, when Tony turned to her. "But Kara has a point. Are you ready to talk about what's on your mind, Brenda?"

Brenda froze. She closed her eyes lightly and moistened her lips. Tony has no right to do this to me. I told him I'd deal with this alone, she protested inwardly. She opened her eyes and met Tony's concerned face. Suddenly she realized he wasn't asking her to talk just for herself. Kara needed to know she could trust Brenda, that Brenda wasn't so very different from her, even though she was working at Garfield as a counselor. She had to show Kara that sharing problems with a group of peers and trying to work them out was what Garfield was all about. For Kara's sake, Brenda nodded.

She faced Kara directly and said, "Thanks for that. I deserved it. I'm having a lot of trouble.

102

Some of the kids here know all the gory details." She turned to Matt, who was in on the session working with a boy that a local drug rehab program had sent to Garfield. "Everything's on the rocks — with my boyfriend and with school. I thought I could handle it myself, with a little help from my friends."

Matt was sitting scrunched in the corner. A smile flickered across his serious face, and he nodded in encouragement for Brenda to continue.

"But I don't seem to be doing too well. I'm beginning to feel I'm the wrong kind of person for Brad to be with — that he made some kind of crazy mistake choosing me. I've been thinking that he needs another kind of girl to live the life he wants to lead."

Tony arched his eyebrows slightly. "Didn't you have something to do with getting together with Brad, too?"

Brenda colored slightly. "Yeah, I guess we sort of found each other, but I can't help feeling he'd be better off with someone more like my sister — my stepsister, Chris." Brenda explained her feelings during last night's dinner.

Rob, the boy Matt worked with, groaned from the opposite wall and dramatically buried his head in his hands. "Tell me about it. My brother's Phi Beta Kappa at Yale; I'm in remedial reading." The way he said it was so funny everybody started laughing. Even Kara smiled.

As the hilarity died down, Tony looked around, pleased that the tension in the room had lessened considerably. He turned again to Brenda. "Could it be that you're jealous of Chris?" he suggested

103

gently. "Are you afraid of something between her and Brad?"

Brenda's reaction was instantaneous. "No. Not at all. And I'm not jealous of her, not anymore." As she spoke, she knew that was the deepest truth. "I just think she's different from me. She's more like Brad, the kind of person who goes after a certain kind of — I don't know — success, I guess." Her voice trailed off.

"You've got your kind of success, too. We all do. I still have a hard time with that, accepting that what I do with my hands, fixing things, is as important as what someone does who's an artist," Matt admitted, knowing everyone except probably Kara knew about the barrier he had put up at first between him and his girl friend, Pamela.

"Maybe he's not who you need to lead the life you want to lead," Kara half mumbled.

Brenda looked up, startled. Kara didn't sound hostile anymore, just a little afraid, out of her element talking in a group like this. Kara's words stuck in her mind and needled her more than they should have. Mentally Brenda filed Kara's remark away for later. "Thanks, Kara," she said. "I'll think about that."

She pressed her hands to her temples and propped her chin in her hands. She sat in silence for a second, wondering if she would ever figure out what was going on between her and Brad, why suddenly everything about their relationship was coming into question. Dust danced in the sunlight spilling through the tall windows into the pale painted room. Brenda poked her bare foot into the path of the sunbeam and let out a sigh before she spoke again. "About Brad — I think I have to try to talk to him more about my feelings about Garfield and the work here. Make him understand what's important to me." She paused, then faced Kara with a tentative smile. "But the other problem is if I don't pass chemistry with at least a C next week, I don't graduate."

"You're failing chemistry?" Kara said, obviously astounded. "Oh, wow!" She slapped the floor with her hand, threw her head back, and chuckled. Brenda was surprised to see how pretty Kara looked when she laughed. "Why didn't you say so? I mean, I'm great at chemistry; I can help you. Everyone I've ever tutored passed. Besides, I aced McQuarrie's exam last semester myself." The note of pride in her voice was unmistakable.

Brenda didn't quite know how to respond. She was shocked at first, then remembered reading Kara's file in Tony's office. Kara Wakely was some kind of science whiz, a real brain, who kept dropping out of one exclusive private boarding school after another. Now that she lived at home with her parents and went to Kennedy, she had taken to running away from home. She obviously couldn't get used to her parents' presence and discipline, she was so used to living without them. She was, however, unusually gifted and sensitive.

Out of the corner of her eye, Brenda could see Tony watching her closely. She realized that here was a real chance to help somebody, to help *two* somebodies! Brenda's face broke into a free, happy smile. "I'd like that, Kara, a lot. Believe me, I can use all the help I can get."

"And it mightn't be a bad thing if some of it didn't come from Brad," Tony interjected.

Brenda stared questioningly at the youth counselor, but Tony deftly turned the rap session in a different direction, leaving her wondering if he was right.

"The most incredible thing just happened!" Brenda announced in a loud whisper. She had just located Brad in the reference section of the Rose Hill Library. She sat down beside him at the long oak table and regarded him with shining eyes.

Brad put a finger to his lips and nodded over his shoulder toward the card catalog where Mrs. Mavis, the librarian, was looking in their direction.

Brenda bit her lip and stifled a giggle. She shoved her bracelet up further on her arm, and leaned closer to Brad. "One of the kids at Garfield, the girl I'm counseling — "

"Carol?"

"Kara," Brenda corrected, vaguely annoyed that Brad still couldn't remember the girl's name. "Well, she's a real science whiz, and she going to tutor me — not that I won't study with you, too," she added hastily, not wanting Brad to get the idea she didn't want him to help her.

Brad pulled back slightly. "So?"

Brenda was all patience as she explained, "Don't you see, Tony's been trying to break through to her for almost a month now. Nothing's worked. Now she up and volunteers to help me."

When Brad didn't respond, Brenda went on

106

to explain. "And that helps her. She'll get her self-esteem back. And I'll have a chance to reach her."

"Brenda," Brad said quietly. "Do you realize in less than a week you have your chem final, and all you can talk about is what happened today at Garfield?"

"Haven't you been listening?" Brenda raised her voice in exasperation. The librarian rattled some papers at the front desk. Brenda arched her eyebrows and leaned even closer to Brad. She dropped her voice to a whisper and said, "Can't you see how important this is? Of course I want to talk about it — and incidentally, it *does* have to do with chemistry." Hearing the edge in her voice, Brenda drew her breath in sharply and resumed in a more playful tone, "Hey, you sound like you're jealous that some-one else is going to help me." She closed her fingers over Brad's and waited for him to smile.

He continued to look grim. Tilting his chair back at a dangerous angle, he folded his arms behind his head and said ruefully, "I don't get it. I mean, all this work you've done at Garfield. You've learned a lot from it, but Brenda, it's al-most over now. I mean, high school's finished for you. It's time to move on. You've got to take charge of your own life."

"What are you saying?" Brenda gasped.

Brad eased his chair back down and brought his face close to hers. His brown eyes were filled with concern. "Don't you see, if you want to help people so much, you have to prepare your-self — professionally. Like I'm doing now. At

Princeton all I have time to do, practically, is study. I can't even volunteer at the local hospital, at least not until I'm a junior. The work load is too heavy. But eventually that will all change. Right now your job is school, not Garfield. You've barely cracked a book yet for that test, and still all you can talk about is how you're helping Kara."

Brenda reacted angrily. "Brad, without Garfield, I would have dropped out of school two years ago. I wouldn't be here trying to pass McQuarrie's stupid final. I don't know where I'd be, but it wouldn't be someplace very pleasant, that's for sure." She gave her pencil an annoyed shove. It rolled off the edge of the table and clattered noisily onto the floor.

"People are trying to work!" A loud whisper sounded at Brenda's elbow.

She looked up guiltily right into the face of the librarian. Mrs. Mavis added in a cross voice, "If you two have so much talking to do, I'd appreciate it it you would take your conversation outside, where it belongs."

Brenda pursed her lips and glared at the retreating form of the woman. Brad's next words made her sit up with a start. "She's right," he whispered, beginning to stack Brenda's books. "Let's get out of here."

"That would suit me just fine!" Brenda said aloud. She flashed the librarian a defiant look as she traipsed across the room and out the front door.

"I can't believe this!" Brad looked over his shoulder in annoyance.

"She really was a drag!" Brenda commented, hoisting herself up on a low-ivy-covered retaining wall.

"She was right. I can't believe we were actually having an argument in the library." Brad glared at Brenda, then dumped her books beside her and leaned back against the cool stones.

Brenda rolled her eyes. Sometimes Brad's tendency to live by the letter of the law drove her crazy. "It seems to me you might be more upset about the idea we were having an argument." Little forests of moss grew up between the cracks in the top of the stone wall. Brenda dug at one patch with the tip of her finger.

Brad put his hand over hers. "It's dumb to argue about stuff like this."

"Dumb?" Brenda repeated. A warning bell somewhere deep inside her head said shut up. This isn't the time to discuss Garfield with Brad. Brenda chose to ignore it. "I don't think it's dumb to defend what's important to me," she said, knowing she was baiting him, desperately not wanting to, but even more desperately wanting to get these crazy feelings inside out into the open.

Brad folded his arms across his chest and stared sullenly across the parking lot. "So, talk about it," he said, a note of hostility in his voice. "But remember, the whole time you talk about it, we aren't getting any work done." He turned around and faced Brenda head-on. Exasperation was written all over his face. "Don't you want to graduate?"

"How can you ask something like that? Of

course I do. Just because I think differently from you — or Chris — " Brenda drew in her breath sharply. "That's it, isn't it? I figured it all out last night, at that dinner. I'm all wrong for you. What you need is somone like Chris."

"Like Chris?" Brad's annoyed expression darkened to anger. "What does Chris have to do with this. With you and me? She's not the Austin I go out with. You are. And you're the Austin who might not graduate ten days from now. I just want to help you."

Brenda stroked her hair back off her forehead and leaned forward. "I'm just the wrong person for someone like you." Her voice grew hesitant. "It's been that way all along. I just haven't seen it until now." She turned toward Brad and looked at him with wide, sad eyes. "I thought loving someone made none of that matter."

"What are you saying?" The anger was gone from Brad's voice. He suddenly sounded very scared. "What does our relationship have to do with studying for your exam?" He gave her shoulders a gentle shake. "Brenda, you're not making sense."

"Yes, I am," she said, slipping down off the wall and standing face-to-face with him. "No matter how I try to explain to you what's important to me, you just can't hear. It's as if you're from a different country — a different planet. A place where people plan and plan for the future. Someday you'll help people, but I can't put it off for four years. Why should I, anyway, when I have the chance to help them now?"

"Because you'll be able to do a better job and

110

help in bigger ways with proper training," Brad said almost glibly. To Brenda it sounded like he was reading from some kind of rule book.

She stared at him in disbelief. "That's not always so," she exclaimed, thinking of Tony and how, single-handedly, he had made Garfield as successful as it was. He hadn't even been to college. What was Brad talking about? "I don't know what happens four years from now, but right now there's work to be done. I can't do much yet with people. I don't have the experience, but just having Kara help me, trusting her and getting her to trust me, giving her a chance to feel like she has something to give, is pretty important to me. As a matter of fact, it's about the most important thing that's happened in my life in weeks. Can't you understand that?"

"No," Brad said flatly. He kicked a loose stone across the pavement. "It seems to me the most important thing in your life right now is the possibility of flunking out of school. And I think you aren't facing up to how scared you are about it. One minute you're talking about helping people. The next minute you're talking about Chris and how she's better suited for me. I think you're pretty mixed up, Brenda, and maybe you should shine some of your honesty on yourself for a change."

"Look who's talking," Brenda retorted, suddenly blurting out her worst fears. "You're the one who should check out what's going on inside." She tapped his chest angrily with her finger. "First you're embarrassed because I might fail a course and not graduate. Heaven forbid Brad

Davidson's girl friend doesn't get her high school diploma. Now you're embarrassed because we fought in the library. What that librarian thought is far more important than what we were talking about — us."

"Us?" Brad growled. "All I know about us these days is every time we're together you keep accusing me of not wanting to be with you, of not understanding who you are. To tell you the truth, you're beginning to make me wonder. I loved Brenda Austin, the girl I left behind last year. But I haven't seen her around lately, I'll tell you that."

"What do you mean?" Brenda challenged, a cold knot of fear forming in her chest.

Brad slicked back his hair with his hands and stared in confusion at Brenda. "I don't know exactly." He paused thoughtfully. "It's just that last year you seemed so directed. You got into Sarah Lawrence. You had a sensible future planned. Now all of a sudden you're acting lost. You're sabotaging yourself over this exam, and no matter how I try to tell you, you don't listen."

"Lost?" Brenda sputtered. "I know exactly where I want to go. I've just finished telling you a hundred times what my direction is. And you don't listen to me, Brad, because my direction is different from yours." Brenda cut herself off. The awful truth of what she had just said struck her for the first time. Maybe this was what had been different between her and Brad since his return from Princeton. He was walking down the road, his eyes focused on some goal far off in the sunset, and she was still here in Rose Hill, already living the most important part of her dreams, and Brad couldn't accept that. "The real problem between us, Brad, is you just don't seem to understand me. That's all the help I need from you right now — for you to understand. But you don't seem to want to try. The future you have in mind for me might not be what I want. It might not be what's right for me. What I want is here, and I'm lucky enough to be doing what I want to do with my life right now."

Brad threw his hands up in the air. "I give up. If what you want to do with your life is goof off, then goof off. Play counselor at Garfield. Throw away four years of high school. That's up to you, Brenda. But I don't want any part of it."

"Don't worry. You won't *be* any part of it," Brenda shouted. She grabbed her books from the wall and met Brad's angry glance. "I don't need your help studying anymore. And I am beginning to think I don't need you." With that Brenda whirled around and started down the block on the long walk home. As far as she was concerned, Brad Davidson was the last person in the world she ever needed to see again.

# *Chapter*
# *11*

$F$our blocks later the truth sank in. *I've just broken up with Brad!* Brenda's hand flew to her chest, and she stopped dead in her tracks. She stood very still, trying to catch her breath. She hadn't meant for their argument to go that far. The cold hard knot inside her began to break up, and Brenda felt a familiar tug at the back of her throat. Stifling the sob that rose to her lips, she bolted into the nearby entrance of Rosemont Park.

She hurried down the side paths, away from the old mansion and formal gardens at the center of the park. A lazily flowing stream flanked by dark pines and tall willows came into view. Brenda ducked under a droopy willow branch and sank down on the cool damp ground, burying her face in her arms. But the tears stayed locked inside her as if they were hard and frozen. The enormity of what she had just done struck her with full force. She had thrown away the only real love she'd ever known in her life. She had thought that their love was stronger than the problems that could come between her and Brad. But obviously Brenda wasn't quite up to knowing how to love someone yet.

Uttering a low moan, she sat up and tossed a pebble into the stream. She watched the rings spread around it and thought about how she was still ruining everything she touched. Who had she been kidding? She was just as messed up now as she had been two years ago. Nothing, nothing at all, had changed in her life. Brad was reaching out to her, wanting to help, and she was pushing him away. In a flash Brenda was sure that's what she'd just done. Pushed Brad away because being near him next year meant things might get really serious between them. Brenda wrapped her arms around her legs and leaned her head way back. What was wrong with her? Was she always going to run away from the people she loved?

From deep down inside her a voice seemed to answer. No. No, she wasn't going to run away. She wasn't running away now. Brenda stretched her legs out in front of her and stared at her black hightops. Slowly her pulse began to slow down, and her world began to come back into focus. With great effort she tried to recapture the events of the last hour or so: talking to everyone at Garfield, Kara reaching out to help her, then meeting Brad. No, she hadn't made a mistake just now. Oh, maybe it was the wrong way, the wrong time to break things off. But the reasons for leaving him had been right. He really didn't understand what her life was about. He expected her to live according to his own guidelines: go to college for four years, then graduate school or whatever, then become a psychologist. He kept reminding her how good she'd be at that. But sensible as it all sounded, that was Brad's way of doing things, not hers.

The lump in the back of Brenda's throat began to dissolve, and quietly, burying her face in her hands, she began to cry.

She didn't hear the sound of a twig breaking underfoot, and Phoebe calling her name twice, very softly, before Brenda looked up.

"Phoebe?" Brenda hastily wiped her arm across her face. "What are you doing here?"

Phoebe stood there hesitantly, not sure whether she should go or leave. "I — I needed to be alone for a while. Hey, are you okay?" she asked.

Brenda gave a short, ironic laugh. "I've been better." Looking at Phoebe's red-rimmed eyes, she said, "Hey, you've been better, too." She patted the ground beside her.

Phoebe gave a small smile and settled herself beside her friend. "I'll be okay, I guess. Actually, I feel pretty dumb," Phoebe admitted. She dug into her bag, and her hand emerged with a fistful of career brochures. "I just might have blown my whole relationship with Michael over this!" She shoved the fliers in Brenda's face. "Actually, I came here to tear these into little pieces and float them down the river."

"Sasha wouldn't approve of that," Brenda said lightly, gesturing toward the brownish water.

"You'll pollute the sacred stream, or whatever she used to call this when she was a kid."

In spite of her mood, Phoebe giggled. "Right. I guess I'd better not do that." She recounted the details of her argument with Michael. "I just feel so abnormal," she finished up, "not being anything in particular. Not knowing who I am, what I'm meant for." She sighed.

Brenda cracked a smile. "There's nothing abnormal about not having your whole life mapped out in front of you. You're only seventeen. There's so much more to learn about before you make that kind of decision," she said wisely.

Phoebe considered Brenda's words carefully. "Well, that is the most sensible thing anyone's said to me in days," she said slowly. "And I guess I'll have to live with that. In fact, I'm going to have to since I can't figure out what else to do." Her face lighted up with a smile that quickly gave way to a frown. "But what about Michael?"

Brenda leaned forward and tugged Phoebe's braid. "Everyone has fights now and then. They aren't the end of the world." Brenda's voice shook slightly, but she gained control and continued more steadily. "You'll work things out with Michael. He's probably just hurt because you made such a big decision without him."

"Such a *dumb* decision," Phoebe groaned, flopping back on the ground. She stared up through the leaves at the clear summer sky. "Can you picture me a forest ranger?" Part of her hoped Brenda wouldn't laugh, but she did.

"No," Brenda gasped finally. "Not at all. Do

you really want to wear a hat like Smokey the Bear?"

Phoebe stared at her amazed, then cracked up. "I hadn't thought of that."

Finally their laughter subsided. Phoebe propped her head on her hand and looked at Brenda. "What about you?" she prodded gently. "You didn't exactly look too happy when I walked up," she said carefully.

Brenda hopped to her feet and dusted off her pants. Tucking her hands into her back pockets she walked a little way toward the stream. When she turned around, her eyes were bright with tears. "I just broke up with Brad."

Phoebe straightened up. "What! What happened?" she gasped as soon as she found her voice.

"I suppose I should be relieved that you look so shocked," Brenda quipped. "I was beginning to think everyone had noticed how we just didn't fit together very well anymore. Ever since he came back from college." Her voice quavered.

Phoebe frowned. "I never felt that. Not at all. In fact, you seemed so happy together lately." Seeing the pain on Brenda's face, Phoebe cut herself off. She jumped to her feet and hurried to Brenda's side.

"Do you want to talk about it?" she asked gently, putting a hand on Brenda's arm.

Brenda shrugged her shoulders and gave a tight little shake of her head. "I tried to talk to Brad. It didn't work." She bit her lip and sniffed back her tears. "He just doesn't understand me," she began slowly. "I know it sounds trite, but every-

118

one else I know seems to feel that what I want to do with my life is right. But not Brad. Today I felt like I was talking to someone who lived in some distant galaxy. Phoebe," Brenda cried passionately, "he felt *that* far away. But during the rap session today at Garfield, I felt so close to everyone. No one thought the way I want to live my life was weird or out of sync. Only Brad thinks that. He wants me to become someone else, someone driven, ambitious. Someone like Chris."

Phoebe understood what Brenda meant. "Maybe you're not meant to live by the same set of rules as Brad Davidson. Brad's a wonderful guy, but sometimes he's got blinders on."

Brenda nodded. She wiped away the tears that stubbornly insisted on rolling down her cheeks. "You know, he's the one person I can't talk to."

"Sounds to me like you've got some serious communication problems," Phoebe said, but added cautiously, "but that doesn't mean you should give up. You two have been so good together."

Phoebe's words reduced Brenda to another bout of tears. Phoebe instantly threw her arms around her friend and stroked her dark head until gradually Brenda's sobs died down. "Give it another chance, Bren," Phoebe whispered.

Brenda just nodded. "I — I'll try, Phoebe. Meanwhile, that chem test is next week. I'd better get home to study. Graduation, not Brad, is really my biggest problem right now."

"Need a ride?" Phoebe offered, not wanting to see Brenda go off alone.

Brenda accepted gladly. As she climbed into

the rusty green station wagon, Brenda realized she was holding Phoebe's brochures. "How'd I get these?" she asked.

"Oh, give them to me." Phoebe opened the glove compartment. Before she stuffed them in, she changed her mind. "Hey, Brenda," she said, her voice bright with excitement. "I just thought of something. One of these brochures might have the answer to all your problems."

"Now, Phoebe," Brenda cautioned.

"Really." Before starting the car, Phoebe swung around in her seat and crossed her legs. She faced Brenda squarely and said, "Working things out with Brad is one thing you have to figure out for yourself. But I think one of your problems might be that you don't want to go to college at all."

"But I have to if I want to become a therapist."

"I know that. But you don't have to go to college immediately." Phoebe paused to riffle through the fliers. "Here, look at this."

Brenda eyed it skeptically. " 'Work Study Programs at Georgetown University,' " she read aloud.

"You want to help people now. You have the offer of a job at Garfield. Why don't you take it and go to school part-time or at night. In work-study programs you get college credit for the work you do. I'm sure there's a plan that will work for you at Georgetown, or somewhere around here."

Listening to Phoebe, Brenda's expression slowly changed. "What an incredible idea." Brenda regarded Phoebe with new respect. "I think maybe you're the one who should be a counselor!" She gave Phoebe's overall straps a friendly tug.

Phoebe turned on the ignition and giggled. "Don't let Michael hear you say that. I think the career changes of Phoebe Hall over the past two days are something he'd prefer to forget."

Brenda pocketed the brochure. "So, before we head home," she suggested as they pulled out of the park onto Rosemont Boulevard, "let's go somewhere and work out a game plan. I'm going to have to present your brilliant idea to Daddy Austin, and I think I'd better have the details pretty straight in my head before I do."

"To Mario's?" Phoebe asked.

"Mario's!" Brenda answered, hoping she wouldn't run into Brad there.

# *Chapter*
## *12*

For dessert Friday night, Brenda baked her stepfather's favorite chocolate cake. She put it on her mother's best glass serving dish and garnished the plate with rosebuds from the garden. When she brought it into the dining room, she avoided Chris's eyes. She hadn't told her anything yet about her decision, though she knew the cake was a dead giveaway that something big was in the works. Astute Chris would realize that instantly. Their father, as Brenda had hoped, was completely oblivious of the fact that Brenda was trying to put him in a mellow, receptive mood.

"Brenda, how thoughtful!" Jonathan Austin said, helping himself to a generous portion.

"It's beautiful, dear," her mother complimented, arching her eyebrows and regarding her daughter with some curiosity.

After a nervous gulp, Brenda managed a smile. Chris passed her a hefty slice of cake. "Thanks,"

Brenda said, poking at the thick, dark frosting with the prongs of her fork and mustering up her courage to speak. For a few minutes the only sound around the elegant oval table was the clink of forks against porcelain plates.

"Uh, Dad," Brenda said at last, breaking the silence in a barely audible voice.

Her stepfather looked up from the head of the table with a satisfied smile.

Brenda forced herself to speak louder. "I'd like to talk to you about something."

A flicker of suspicion crossed her stepfather's chiseled face. "Then, this, I take it, is a bribe," he said with a narrow smile, helping himself to another serving.

"Well, at least it's a bribe we're all enjoying," Chris said brightly. Brenda knew Chris must have thought she was about to spill the beans about her problems with chemistry and graduation. Well, she'd be as surprised as her parents when she heard her sister's new plan.

"What I've got to say concerns all of you — my whole family," Brenda stressed.

Her mother slowly put down her fork. Brenda watched her struggle not to look too upset. She didn't miss the worried glance her parents exchanged, a look she hadn't seen in a long time. For a moment Brenda panicked. Here I go again, she thought, the black sheep of the family about to upset the Austin applecart. Then she forced back the old familiar feeling of rebellion, of wanting to push her chair back from the table, jump up, and bolt out of the room. She twisted the white linen napkin tightly in her hands and met her stepfather's eyes. They were the purest blue, just like Chris's. "I've just made a decision that I'd like to share with all of you." She paused and took a deep breath. "I don't want to go to college next year." There, she'd said it. It was out in the open. She held her breath, waiting for a reaction.

Instead of exploding, her stepfather just frowned. "I don't understand. What changed your mind?" He sounded puzzled, but not angry, not critical. Brenda looked at Chris. She looked as surprised as her parents, but encouraged Brenda with a smile.

"It's not that I don't want to go to college, exactly. It's just that I want to go part-time, or at night, and work at Garfield House full-time." Before her stepfather could say a word, Brenda barreled on, keeping her eyes focused on the untouched piece of cake on her plate. "I spoke to Tony today. He offered me a real job there. It won't pay much, but I'll be doing what I want to do, helping the kids there. Getting hands-on training."

"It sounds like what you need is a work-study program somewhere," her stepfather said, smoothing his faded blond hair. "What do you think?" He turned toward Brenda's mother. Her high-cheekboned face was bathed in a huge smile.

"I think that's a wonderful idea."

"You do?" Brenda's chin jutted forward, and her eyes popped open very wide.

Her stepfather took a long sip of coffee, then said slowly, "I suppose we should have shared this with you sooner, but I want you to know how proud we are of how far you've come over the past couple of years. I was stubborn at first. I didn't want to believe that that halfway house was a major factor in helping you change. But it was. And working there, I think you've blossomed into quite a remarkable young lady — "

"Dad!" Chris jumped in, then stopped herself quickly.

Jonathan Austin flashed his daughter an apologetic look. "Excuse me, Chris. I mean a remarkable young woman. Four years of college right after high school aren't necessarily for everyone. I think you're fortunate, Brenda, having found what you want to do so soon in life. I almost envy you that."

Brenda's eyes filled with tears. She jumped up from her seat and hurried to her stepfather's side. Impulsively she threw her arms around his neck, rumpling his starched collar and twisting his tie. Her relationship with her stepfather was usually pretty reserved, because she knew displays of emotion confused him. But at the moment she didn't care. She planted a quick happy kiss on his balding head, then leaned back and regarded him with shining eyes. "I feel so incredibly lucky to be part of this family. To have you as my father."

Her stepfather's face worked emotionally for a fleeting second, then he regained control and tugged at the knot in his tie. "Well, we're all lucky to have you, too. Uh, right, Chris?" he said a bit stiffly.

Chris was beaming. She glanced from her

father to Brenda to her stepmother, then back to Brenda again. "You said it!" she declared, wiping a tear from the corner of her eye.

Jonathan Austin cleared his throat and said in a no-nonsense voice, "But as lofty as all this sounds, I would like to hear a bit about the practical details, miss!" He looked sternly at Brenda as he ticked the points off his fingers. "Where will you live? Here or in an apartment or at Garfield? How much money will you make, and what definite plans are you going to make for your education? I think you realize that to continue in counseling work you'll need a degree."

Brenda tried to stop smiling and look serious. She explained her plans to her family, recounting parts of her long discussion with Tony earlier that day. She had thought she would live at Garfield, but Tony said no. She'd need a life of her own outside the halfway house. A place away from the kids and their problems. A place to study. If it was still okay, she'd live at home, even paying rent if they wanted her to. But later on, when she saved some money, she'd like to have her own apartment. She had an appointment with the school counselor next week, but she had read about a couple of programs at D.C. area colleges that could be tailored to suit her needs and work schedule.

"And what does Brad say about all this?" Brenda's mother asked a little later as the girls did the dishes in the kitchen.

Brenda closed her eyes and pushed down the

126

cold, scary feeling inside that threatened to emerge. She wasn't ready to talk about Brad yet, or what had happened between them.

Chris came to her rescue. "Well, whatever he thinks, Brenda has to live her own life, doesn't she, Mom?" Chris sought Brenda's eyes.

From the sad expression on Chris's face, Brenda knew that the crowd's grapevine had been buzzing. Brenda wasn't sure yet if the relationship was really over, but already her breakup with Brad was pretty much public knowledge. Deep down inside that scared her even more.

# *Chapter*
# *13*

"You really took that awful batch of aptitude tests — and you didn't *have* to?" Chris exclaimed, waving her right hand in the air trying to get her nail polish to dry. She, Sasha, and Phoebe were gathered in the Jenkins' town house for their last-ever slumber party.

"What ever possessed you to do a thing like that?" Sasha asked, poking her head out of the hall closet. She was standing tiptoe on the top of the step stool looking for her mother's old plastic hair rollers.

Phoebe complacently bit into one of Sasha's carob nut brownies and munched a while before answering her friends. She was enjoying herself too much to rush through her account. Not until she divulged the details of her visit to Ms. Murdock in the counseling office did she realize what a funny story it made. She looked up at Chris and grinned. "I took every test invented. And I aced them all!" Phoebe giggled and selected some bright blue nail polish from the row of bottles lined up on the kitchen table.

Sasha hopped down from the stool and deposited a large Christmas cookie tin on the table next to the jars and tubes of makeup and cosmetics. "How'd you do that?" she inquired as she pried open the gaily painted lid. Jumbo pink foam rubber rollers bounced out.

"Wow, I remember these. They must be antiques!" Chris squealed, gingerly poking one with a finger. She waved a roller in Phoebe's face. "But before we get distracted with trying to remember exactly how we set our hair when we were twelve years old, I think you'd better explain yourself. No one aces aptitude tests. They aren't scored that way."

Phoebe answered smugly. "Sorry, Ms. President, but you're dead wrong. I really did ace them. I am equally good at absolutely everything — well, *almost* everything — apparently I wouldn't make a good car mechanic!" She emitted a dramatically gloomy sigh. "But," she added, a glint lighting up her green eyes. "I would make a top-notch farmer — "

"Farmers these days are in a bad way. Didn't you see the Farm Aid concert?" politically minded Sasha broke in.

Phoebe waved aside her concerns. " — Or an astronaut!"

"You're kidding!" Chris squinted at her skeptically. "What kind of test was this?"

"A very good kind. The very best. It told me everything I needed to know about myself. And

I think Ms. Murdock learned a few things, too." Phoebe chuckled evilly. She carefully licked each bit of gooey carob off her fingers and sniffed the air.

"The brownies!" Sasha screeched. She dashed across the cozy kitchen of her family's town house, reached for a pot holder, and poked her dark head into the oven. "Saved — just in the nick of time," she declared, and put the pan on a rack to cool.

"But, Phoebe," Chris said earnestly, "I don't think these tests helped you at all. If you are good at everything, how can you possibly know what to do with your life?"

Phoebe opened the nail polish and began working on her left hand. Already her pinky was painted metallic gold, her thumb shocking pink. She poked out her index finger and began brushing on the cobalt blue liquid. "Ms. Murdock said I should go into something creative."

Chris and Sasha eyed each other and exclaimed in unison, "Like theater or music!"

Phoebe let out a lovely laugh. It was so wonderful being here tonight with her oldest best friends. "What a great idea this slumber party was!" she said with a warm look at each of them. Then she continued, "But Brenda said something more important. She told me that not knowing what to do yet was fine, that I should just go ahead and walk into college knowing I've got four years to discover what's right for me." Phoebe's smile dimmed a little as she admitted, "Michael tried to tell me that, too." She looked down at her feet. She was wearing her furry rabbit slippers. She bent over and twiddled one of the frayed ears. When she looked up again, her eyes were bright with tears.

The other girls fell silent. Sasha got up and started brushing Phoebe's long hair. "Don't wait too long to call him, Phoebe, and tell him you're sorry about what happened the other day," she advised, picking up a roller and winding it close to Phoebe's head. Phoebe let herself enjoy the sensation of Sasha playing with her hair. She suddenly felt like a little girl, only she wasn't so sure that in the morning everything would be all right the way it always was when you were a kid. She sniffed back her tears and handed Sasha the next roller.

"I guess I feel kind of silly. Sometimes I just act so dumb!" she groaned, reaching for the face cream. "Did we really put all this gunk on when we were twelve?" She eyed the white contents dubiously. "This looks like the ingredients for a classic case of acne!"

Chris nodded solemnly. "Yeah, we were all dumb then, too." She laughed and gave Phoebe's sleeve a tug. "I wouldn't make such a big deal out of what happened with Michael. You two will work it out. But Sasha is right. I wouldn't let it go too long."

"Don't worry, Chris, I won't," Phoebe said with a determined shake of her head.

"Is that what happened with Brenda and Brad?" Sasha asked.

Phoebe felt the mood in the room change. It was always like that when one of the couples in the crowd broke up. Everyone else got a little

131

edgy and nervous, as if breakups were somehow contagious. She gave a little shiver and promised herself to talk to Michael first thing in the morning.

"I don't think so," Chris answered Sasha. "I think it's been coming for a long time." She drew her legs up, tucking her bare feet primly under the hem of her blue-flowered nightgown. "I don't think Brenda realizes how much she's changed this past year. She thinks it's all Brad," Chris said, sounding a little uncomfortable. Sharing Brenda's secrets with her friends was something she hadn't done in a long time. "But I'm not sure it's really over between them. They're going through a rough spot. It's hard being apart like that for a whole year." She cast a meaningful glance at Phoebe, who just nodded in response. Phoebe's old boyfriend, Griffin Neill, had moved to New York. When he came home again, things began to fall apart between them.

A loud noise followed, and the sound of laughter on the back porch made all the girls sit up. "What was that?" Phoebe asked in a frightened whisper.

"I don't know." Sasha's hushed answer turned into a shriek as the back door burst open. "WHAT ARE YOU DOING HERE!"

"GREG!" Chris screamed, pulling her old chenille bathrobe tight across her chest. Then she remembered the cream on her face and her half-set hair, and she groaned.

"Michael!" Phoebe barely could get the word out. She stood there staring at him. He had the most extraordinary expression on his face. "Phoebe, what have you done to your face?" Michael whooped, then doubled over with laughter.

"Rob Kendall, what are you doing here!" Sasha planted her hands on her hips and tapped her slippered foot angrily on the floor. A ring of curlers circled the ends of her naturally wavy dark hair, and her face was covered with a film of organic green clay masque. Still, she stood up very straight and tried as hard as she could to look dignified.

The boys all answered at once, and nothing they said made sense. "So this is a girls' slumber party." Michael just stood there grinning, looking Phoebe up and down, paying particular attention to her curlers. "Colorful!" he chuckled.

"When I went to the Albatross to look for you, your parents told me all about this. I thought you'd enjoy a little male company!" Rob's eyes twinkled behind his glasses.

"Enough preliminaries. We've decided to have a prefinals come-as-you-are party," Greg concluded, "and you three are the guests of honor. Come on now, let's go right out the door. The car is right outside. Morty has a six-foot sub waiting at the sub shop." He clapped his hands together, then headed toward Chris. She was shrinking back into a corner, looking horrified.

"Oh, no!" she exclaimed, shielding her face. "I'm not going anywhere. Not like this!"

"Oh, yes, you are!" Greg said in a commanding tone. Before Chris could react, he had scooped her up in his strong arms and was carrying her, screeching and kicking, toward the door. "Okay, guys, do your thing. Onward to the sub shop!"

"THE SUB SHOP!" Chris's yell filled the night. "Put me down. I'm not going to the sub shop like this. Greg, I'll — I'll — " Chris's protests faded as Greg walked outside where more shouts and cheers greeted him.

Phoebe cringed. The whole crowd was here — somewhere.

Sasha marched past Rob into her parents' bedroom. She emerged a second later carrying a huge terry cloth robe. "I am *not* leaving this house in just my nightie," she said. She plunged her arms into the flowing sleeves and stomped out the door into the dark, Rob following close behind her, his laughing voice trailing back into the kitchen. "Sash, don't be mad. I can explain everything."

Phoebe didn't know what to do. She stood awkwardly in the kitchen, half wishing the floor would open up and swallow her, half praying Michael would just run up and kiss her and tell her everything was okay. Of course, the fact he was here had to mean something.

Michael seemed embarrassed, too. He looked around the cluttered room and whistled under his breath, "What a mess."

"We were just trying to reenact one of our junior high sleepovers. That's all." Phoebe gestured with her head toward the butcher block counter. Sasha's cassette of sixties and seventies favorites was still in the tape deck. The mellow strains of "Yesterday" filled the kitchen. Phoebe approached the tape player and turned it off.

"We'd better close up before we join the crowd," Michael said.

Phoebe just nodded. She knew she should wipe the cream off her face, do something to look more presentable. But that wouldn't be fair. Sasha and Chris hadn't had a chance to.

"Are — are there a lot of people?" she asked in a whisper. She tugged on the top of her candy-striped pajamas. She had worn them as a joke. Now she felt terribly self-conscious and very unattractive.

Michael turned away from latching the window and just grinned. "Come on out and see. This is a come-as-you-are party." He held out his hand.

Phoebe took it shyly. Halfway to the door, Michael stopped. He looked down at Phoebe with a tender expression on his face. With a tentative finger, he poked at the cream covering her nose. "Weird stuff," he said.

Phoebe looked down at her slippers. "I'm sorry, Michael. About that scene the other day. I *was* overreacting to everything. I feel better now, really I do. I didn't mean to take it out on you."

"Hey, Pheeb!" Michael locked his arms around her waist and leaned back against the wall. "I'm sorry, too. I wasn't exactly sympathetic, was I? You were upset, and that's all that mattered. I didn't take you seriously. I'm beginning to understand now. It's hard leaving all this." He looked around Sasha's cozy living room, then out the front door, where someone was violently honking the horn on his van.

"Hey, what's going on in there!" Bart's voice cut through the dark.

Michael chuckled. "Not what he thinks, that's for sure."

Phoebe started laughing. "I'm sure people don't really kiss with this stuff on." She wrinkled her nose. The cream felt sticky and cold on her skin, and she was beginning to think all this twelve-year-old stuff was something she was mighty glad to have grown out of.

"That's what you think," Michael said, lowering his face over hers.

"Michael, I look so yucky!" Phoebe squirmed to get free, then met Michael's eyes. The protest died on her lips.

The horn honked again. Phoebe pulled back from him, laughing. "Sasha's parents are going to get in trouble with the neighbors!" she warned, not making a move toward the door. She reached up and tenderly wiped a dab of cream off Michael's cheek.

Michael rolled his eyes and led her toward the door. "So, tell me, are you really going to Cornell?"

Phoebe pretended to consider her answer. "Well, I guess not. Tonight I've decided I'm not going to be a forest ranger after all." She paused for effect, then continued, "But I might stay right here in Washington."

Michael stopped in his tracks.

Phoebe pretended not to notice. She kept on walking and said as casually as she could, "I was thinking of going to Georgetown for political science. You know, to prepare myself for a career as an aide in the White House of Madame President Chris Austin!"

Michael slapped his hand against the door frame and howled, "You do that, Phoebe. You just do that." He slammed the door, then clunked down the front steps onto the walk where Phoebe was waiting. Arm-in-arm they headed for the van, joining in with the rest of the crowd singing the Kennedy Fight Song.

# Chapter
# 14

The Rose Hill Open Air Farmers' Market was bustling. Brad checked his watch. It was hard to believe so many people were actually up and about at seven A.M. on a Saturday morning. He slowed his jog to a walk and pulled the terry cloth sweatband off his head. Stretching his arms over his head, he paced back and forth in front of a cart of dried flowers and herbs, waiting for his pulse to slow down.

He had awakened at the crack of dawn and run the four miles from his house in record time. But he still wasn't tired. He was edgy, restless, and obsessed with trying to figure out exactly what had happened with Brenda. Their nasty little scene in front of the library the other day seemed like some sort of bad dream. All he had wanted to do was help her, and she had pushed him away. She had kept talking about how different they were. But they'd *always* been different. That was one of the reasons Brad loved her. Brenda's warmth, her impulsiveness, her way of rushing into a situation to lend a hand and only later worrying about the consequences — it was those traits that made her special to him. She had a kind of courage Brad had at first admired, now loved. Now suddenly Brenda was saying she needed someone more like her. But the way she said it made it sound like *he* was the one wanting someone else, someone more from his world. Brad was hurt, angry, confused, and scared. He felt Brenda had somehow slipped out of his hands, and he had no idea how to win her back again. He leaned back against the hood of a pickup truck and stared gloomily at his feet.

"Brad, what are you doing here?" Sasha Jenkins cried. Brad looked up, confused. Sasha was wearing a broad-brimmed sun hat and a swirly peasant skirt. She held a wicker basket full of vegetables and flowers. In spite of the hour she looked very much awake, and from the expression on her face, Brad knew she had heard all about him and Brenda. He clenched his fist. Sometimes having so many friends, knowing so many people, wasn't an asset. He felt like nothing in his life was private. Whatever was going on between him and Brenda shouldn't have been anyone else's business.

"I was out for a run," he said, shoving his sweatband down on his forehead and doing some neckrolls. "I was about to run home."

"Oh." Sasha's disappointment was genuine. "I was going to ask you over for breakfast. My mom makes the best pancakes on weekend mornings.

I was just picking up some maple syrup." She motioned toward a cart nearby.

"Can I take a raincheck?" Brad asked, realizing that no matter what Sasha knew, she wasn't judging him in any way. "I've got some things to do this morning, and I've still got a long run home."

"It's a deal. Maybe next week. If that doesn't work, we're going to be around all summer. Just drop into the bookstore; we'll make a date." She smiled warmly, then looked around the town square where the farmers and merchants were doing a brisk business. "Oh, there's the organic grain man!" She clapped her hands in delight. "I'd better hurry and see what he's got. Isn't this place wonderful!" Sasha said, then waved farewell.

It was the flowers that inspired him. The cart next to Sasha's herb man was full of the most beautiful roses Brad had ever seen. They were so fresh the dew clung to the dark red petals. Gently Brad stroked one blossom. It was as soft and downy as Brenda's cheek. The awful feeling he would never see her, never touch her, again overwhelmed him. He unzipped the pocket of his sweatpants and pulled out a ten-dollar bill. He was surprised at how many roses it bought. But it was June, he reasoned, and roses were in full bloom.

Later that afternoon when Brad drove up to the Austins' stately house, no one was home. Chris's blue Chevette wasn't in the driveway, and the doors were locked up tight. Brad wasn't sure what to do. He sat in his silver Honda, looking blankly at the front porch. His plan had seemed so simple that morning. Just turn up without calling. That way Brenda wouldn't have a chance to say no. Just hand her the flowers and tell her he loved her from the bottom of his heart. Brenda would recognize the truth of that. Brad was sure of it.

The sun beat down on the car roof; Brad was sweltering. Reluctantly he turned the ignition on. Sitting here all day roasting to death wasn't going to solve anything. Someone must know where Brenda was. He didn't exactly relish the thought of marching into the sub shop or heading for Mario's and asking the kids if they'd seen her. But if getting Brenda back meant swallowing his pride, he'd do it.

Halfway across town he stopped for gas. The self-serve pumps at the Amoco station were shut down, so he wheeled up to the full-service island. He hopped out of the car to stretch his legs and noticed that the attendant looked vaguely familiar.

"Brad — Brenda's friend, right? How ya doin'?" Matt greeted him cautiously.

"Okay," Brad said tersely. He knew Matt vaguely from Garfield House, and he instinctively liked the hardworking, rugged guy. But at the moment Matt seemed like someone in the opposite camp, someone from the world Brenda kept insisting was her world. A world Brad didn't seem to be part of.

"Fill 'er up?"

"No. Just six-dollars' worth." Brad put his hands in the pockets of his neatly creased pants and leaned back against the car. He glanced at Matt out of the corner of his eye. Matt was wiping the windshield vigorously, humming a familiar blues tune under his breath. Almost against his will Brad asked, "So, have you seen Brenda? I was over at her house just now. She wasn't there."

Matt looked up quickly. He had already spotted the flowers on the front seat of the car. He carefully let the windshield wiper back down and dried his hands on the rag hanging out of the pocket of his coveralls. "I saw her this morning," he said carefully. "At Garfield, studying with Kara. I think her exam's early next week."

Brad's body tensed. The idea of Kara helping Brenda when he couldn't irked him. He fished his money out of his pocket and impatiently watched the meter on the pump. Matt reached across him and expertly clicked off the nozzle as the dollar sign hit six.

He hooked the hose on the side of the pump and hesitated before taking Brad's money. "I hear things aren't going too well between you." Matt regarded Brad with dark, serious eyes.

Brad flinched under Matt's gaze. He was embarrassed and annoyed that Matt knew anything about Brenda and him. He knew his reaction was unreasonable. Matt was one of Brenda's good friends. He worked with her at Garfield and probably even sat in with her on some of the same rap sessions. The idea of Brenda talking about their problems to a group of runaways and Tony and kids he didn't even know from Kennedy made him feel sick.

"Listen," he said hotly, shoving the bills into Matt's hand. "What's between me and Brenda is between me and Brenda. Not between *you* and me and Brenda." He started for the driver's side of the car.

Matt laid a restraining hand on his arm. "I didn't mean it that way. It's just that I care a lot for Brenda — "

Brad looked away to cover his embarrassment as Matt continued in a strong, urgent voice. "You're having trouble communicating. Both of you. I'll say the same thing to you I said to her. Maybe you should try to think out what's going on between you. It might make it easier to work it out. Try to make it happen. You and Brenda are a pretty good thing, you know."

Brad pulled his arm away and yanked open his door. "I came here for gas, not to listen to your advice to the lovelorn, Jacobs." With that he gunned the engine and with a squeal of wheels drove out the far side of the station.

A few blocks from his house he made a U-turn and headed back toward Georgetown. Talking to Matt had bugged him. What was happening with Brenda was his own business. Everyone he knew in Rose Hill seemed to be getting into the act. If not to his face like Matt, then behind his back. But Matt had done him one big favor. Brad knew where Brenda was now. And no matter how peeved he was at Matt, or any of Brenda's friends, he couldn't let that get in his way just now. Too much was at stake. He had to find Brenda fast, before it was too late, and tell her he loved her.

# *Chapter*
# *15*

"Catalyst?" Kara barked.

"Something that brings about a reaction but isn't changed by the reaction itself," Brenda answered promptly.

"Good," Kara said. "But make sure you say a 'chemical' reaction or McQuarrie will take points off. He's like that."

The two girls were curled on a lumpy couch in a sunny corner of the Garfield lounge. Brenda's chemistry notes littered the floor. It was just two days before her final, and they had been studying together the whole afternoon.

"One more question." Kara ran her finger down a sheet of yellow paper covered with her scrawl. "What's conservation of energy?"

Brenda took in a deep breath. She drew her leg up beneath her and pressed her palms to her forehead. Kara cleared her throat and tapped her pencil against the back of the couch. For a moment, Brenda stared at Kara helplessly. Then a sudden glimmer of recognition crossed her face. "I've got it!" she whooped. "I've really got it." She jumped to her feet and stood looking down at Kara. "It's a law that says energy cannot be created or destroyed, it can only be changed in form!" Brenda held her breath a second waiting for Kara's response.

Kara struggled to keep a straight face, but the sparkle in her gray eyes gave her away. She tossed her pencil up toward the ceiling and cheered. "Brenda, you just about aced our sample McQuarrie test!" She scrambled to her feet, and after a short hesitation, threw her arms around Brenda and gave her an awkward hug. "I'm so proud of you."

"Proud of *me*," Brenda cried as she began to gather her books. "Kara, you're the best teacher I've ever had." Brenda almost added "much better than Brad," but even thinking Brad's name right now hurt too much. At this very moment she was far too happy and pleased with herself to allow herself to think of him. Besides, she had vowed absolutely not to let her mind dwell on him and their terrible fight at all — at least not until after the final. If she did, she knew she'd never make it through the next couple of days. And graduating now was more important to her than ever. She had to hold herself together until this was all over. Then she could let herself think how impossible ever getting back together with Brad seemed.

"I think this calls for a celebration!" Kara said, "and I planned just the thing," she added mysteriously, guiding Brenda down the back hall into the roomy communal kitchen.

The rest of the house was quiet, practically deserted on this Saturday afternoon. Most of the kids were off with Tony on one of his famous fishing trips in Potomac Park. Kara sat Brenda down at the table and bustled around the room, finally emerging from the pantry with a container of Sticky Fingers handpacked ice cream and a cookie jar filled with the lumpiest chocolate chip cookies Brenda had ever seen. "I baked them myself," Kara declared, dumping a handful of the slightly burned cookies onto a paper plate and shoving it toward Brenda. Brenda dutifully took one as Kara began serving up the ice cream.

"Have you ever thought of being a teacher?" Brenda asked, watching the thin girl carefully.

"Me?" Kara regarded Brenda cautiously. "No. I always thought I'd be some kind of scientist. That's what I'm good at. Except it gets kind of boring, especially the lab work."

"No people to talk to," Brenda emphasized. The thing she had hated most about science and math until now was that it seemed so far removed from people and life. But Kara had changed her mind about all that. Brenda savored a spoonful of ice cream and said thoughtfully, "But teaching science might be just the thing. You're really good at it. I'm considered a pretty hopeless case, and look what you did after a couple of sessions."

Kara tried to brush off the compliment. "It wasn't me. It's you. You just have a block about chemistry. Lots of kids do. You don't know how

146

to approach it. That's all. But once you get the knack, it's a breeze."

"Well, you *taught* me the knack, Kara. I still wouldn't understand what a catalyst was if you hadn't explained that it's like a group leader in a rap session," Brenda said earnestly, leaning forward across the chipped Formica table.

"Yeah, no one ever thinks of science that way, but the truth is once you find an image or picture from life, the most abstract ideas start to make sense."

"And that's why you should teach," Brenda repeated more firmly. "I think you should sign up next year for tutoring at school. You can help people, people like me, before they start feeling as hopeless as I was."

Kara contemplated what Brenda had said and nodded. "Well, I'll think about that. I do like teaching. And it's nice," she added almost shyly, "being able to help other kids." Her small, serious face lighted up with a smile.

When Brenda left later, after having eaten her fill of cookies and ice cream, she was thinking about how great Kara seemed these days, how much more alive than when she had first turned up at Garfield a frightened, angry girl.

"Brenda?"

She spun around and found herself face to face with Brad. Her stomach did a somersault, and she had the strange sensation she was on a roller coaster ride. She was truly glad to see Brad, but she knew she couldn't afford to let him too close to her just yet. She had to stay away from him for a few more days, then confront the problems they had between them head-on.

Brad's shirt stuck to his damp back, and his hair hung limply over his forehead. He looked tired, as if he hadn't slept much the past few nights. He looked up at Brenda from the bottom of the front steps, a bunch of roses in his hand. Seeing the flowers, she caught her breath. Then she reined in her feelings and said very carefully, trying to sound neutral, "What are you doing here?"

She knew it was a dumb question. Especially after she spotted the roses. They were a deep, dark red, and Brenda longed to touch their velvety petals.

Keeping his eyes on his feet, Brad said very quickly, "I want to apologize. For everything. I haven't been very understanding about you and Garfield and your feelings. I'm sorry." He looked up at Brenda, and she was suddenly afraid he was on the brink of tears. He added very softly, "I don't want to lose you, Brenda. You know that." The pain in his voice cut through her like a knife.

She was sure her heart was going to break. She reached out a hand toward Brad. It would be easy to kiss him now, to feel his strong, sure arms engulf her, to say everything was okay. But it wasn't. There were some big problems between them. Pretending they weren't important or didn't exist wouldn't work anymore. She pulled her hand back. "I think we have to talk. There have been some changes since the other day. A lot's happened."

She led Brad around the side of the building

and onto the back porch. A clothesline sagged between one of the porch posts and the trunk of a straggly sycamore tree, and laundry flapped lazily in the afternoon breeze. Brenda tossed her bag on the porch swing and motioned for Brad to sit down beside her. He hesitated and looked around.

Brenda couldn't resist a low laugh. "Don't worry, you're not in enemy territory," she said. Then she added in a softer tone, "No one's here except Kara, and she's upstairs."

Brad sat down across from Brenda and placed the roses on the seat between them. For a few minutes the only sound was the creak of the swing swaying gently. Finally Brad spoke. "So, what do we have to talk about?" He eyed Brenda uncertainly. "I really meant what I said out front: I am sorry, for everything."

Brenda tucked her legs under her and fingered a small hole in the knee of her pedal pushers. "I was upset — I *am* upset — because you seem to be my one . . ." — she swallowed hard before saying the next word — "friend who doesn't really understand me."

"Brenda — " Brad sounded very hurt.

She stopped him by raising her hand, as if warding off a blow. "No. Listen. This isn't easy for me, you know."

Brad sighed and sat back in his seat. She remembered the time almost a year before when he had been working in a training program at a hospital. They had almost broken up then because Brenda couldn't understand why he was so driven and obsessed with his work and never had time for her. But this was different. Brenda wasn't saying she didn't have time for Brad, because she always would. She only wanted him to understand that Garfield *now*, not some indefinite future helping people later, was what mattered most to her. Brenda continued. "This place is very important to me." She couldn't look at Brad as she said that.

"So I've noticed," Brad said wryly.

Brenda forced herself not to respond to his comment. She continued, determined to make him understand why she had made the decision she had made. "Maybe you have, but you don't accept it." Finally she looked up at him, her eyes pleading for his understanding. Her voice trembled when she went on. "We have different values, you and I. I didn't think it mattered before, but it does."

"Hey, I want to help people as much as you do," Brad cried.

Brenda took a deep breath. She tried to think of this conversation as happening during a rap session at Garfield. She wanted to be honest and clear and not play games with herself or with Brad.

"I know that," she said quietly. "I never said you didn't. But for you, helping people is the goal. Someday, when you've finished medical school, you'll start to save lives, and that's the way it should be." Brenda wanted so much for Brad to see that she understood him.

Brad sprang to his feet. The swing swung crazily as he marched over to the porch rail and stared out across the yard. He turned around and said in a demanding voice, "Then, what's the problem? What's all this stuff about our values being different?"

"I can't wait to help people. I have to do it now. I *am* doing it now. This — here . . ." — she gestured around the yard and porch — "is my life."

Brad looked up at the sky, then back down at Brenda. He crossed over to her side and knelt in front of her. Taking her hands between his, he said very slowly, as if he were talking to a child, "I understand that, Brenda. But I just think you've been going a bit overboard. To me, studying would come first, so I could help people later. If it's different for you, I accept that. If having Kara help you helps her, I accept that, too. I just don't see what this has to do with all these weird vibes between you and me. I really love you."

Brenda looked down into his dark eyes. They were so full of love. She tenderly brushed a stray lock of hair off Brad's forehead and smiled hesitantly. "You mean that, don't you?"

Brad threw his arms around Brenda's waist and pillowed his face on her lap. His voice was muffled as he said, "You know I do."

She mustered up her courage and said softly, "I love you, too, Brad. But I made a decision." She felt his neck and shoulders tense up. "And if we really love each other, I think we can work out the problems."

Brad lifted his head and looked up at her, puzzled.

"I'm not going to college next year."

Brad's mouth fell open. He stared at Brenda in disbelief. "What?"

"I already talked it over with my folks, and they're behind me a hundred percent on this. I'm going to work full-time at Garfield and go to school locally at night. It'll take longer to get my degree, but I'll be doing what I want to do, and that's what really counts."

"You're not going to Sarah Lawrence in September?" Obviously Brad was only registering part of the conversation.

"No. I'm staying here. I'll live at home for the next year or so, until I save some money."

Brad sat back and looked at Brenda as if she were crazy. "I don't believe this. I really don't believe it!" he cried, getting to his feet. He stared down at her, struggling to find something to say, then paced to the far end of the porch and back. "You're ruining your life, and your parents are letting you do it."

"My parents aren't *letting* me do a thing. I'm eighteen, Brad. I can do what I want," she declared hotly. "But *they're* behind me in this all the way. So are Chris and Tony and all my friends. Except, of course, you!" she cried, her voice rising.

"Oh," Brad snarled sarcastically. "Telling you you're wrong about something makes me less of a friend. Well, I'm sorry. I never thought I was supposed to lie to you to make you happy. When we first met, I thought you were a person who really believed in honesty. But when I'm honest, you start telling me I'm the only one who doesn't understand you."

"Honest!" Brenda practically screamed the word. "You don't know what the word means. Try being honest with yourself for starters. You're just freaked out because your girl friend isn't doing the 'right,' the 'expected,' thing for someone dating a dean's list man. Becoming a big academic success doesn't thrill her, and that upsets you very much. Doesn't it?" Brenda stomped over to Brad and grabbed his arm. She forced him to meet her eyes. Her cheeks were burning, and her heart was pounding like crazy. Back down, Brad, please back down! she begged inwardly.

Brad stared at her long and hard, then carefully removed her hand from his arm. His voice was cool and controlled, but his eyes were smoldering. "I can't believe you think that of me. It's not true. I care about you and what you do, but not for my sake. For yours. I don't care what other people think about how you do at school. Or about you hanging out at Garfield House the next few years of your life. But I can't believe you aren't hurting yourself. Until you found out you might not graduate, you were pretty set in your plans. Now you're just running scared. I can deal with that. But I can't deal with the fact that you won't be honest about it, to yourself or to me."

Brad spun away from Brenda and started down the porch steps.

"Brad!" she shouted after him.

He stopped at the foot of the steps but didn't turn around. Keeping his back straight as an arrow, he didn't move a muscle as he waited for her

153

to say something to make him come back.

"I don't want to see you again. Ever." Brenda's voice was low and calm, but tears streaked down her face. Brad never saw them. Without a parting glance, he broke into a run and bolted for the front of the house.

Brenda sank down on the steps and buried her face in her hands, silently crying, listening. At last Brad's car revved up and squealed away from the curb. She heard the tiny Honda shift from first, to second, to third gear. She kept listening until the sounds of Brad's car blended in with the rest of the afternoon traffic. Only then did she begin to sob loudly, her whole thin body shaking.

"Hey, here's my favorite — " Tony's voice broke off. Brenda hadn't heard him come into the yard. She didn't hear him now, shooing the Garfield residents back to the front of the house.

"Brenda?" he sat down beside her on the top step, his short square hand coming to rest solidly on her back. "What happened?"

Brenda just moaned. "Oh, Tony, I ruined it. I just ruined everything." She looked up at the counselor, her beautiful face puffy and pale and contorted with pain. "It's Brad. It's all over. It's — " She broke down again. Tony drew an arm around her and pulled her close. Slowly, calmly, he smoothed his hand over her back.

"Let it out, Brenda. Just let it all out," he said. Having a friend there beside her made the awful empty feeling inside a little less awful. But it didn't take away the pain of knowing the one guy she had really loved was gone. For good.

# Chapter
# 16

Laurie Bennington covered her face with her manicured hands and peeped through her fingers just in time to see Peter Lacey jump onto the sturdy antique dining table and begin his speech. "I can't watch!" she gasped, giving a miserable little shiver and burying her face in Dick Westergard's shirt. Dick was laughing so hard, he wasn't much comfort. The only thing that made Laurie feel a little better was that Peter had taken his shoes off before getting up on the table.

"This is hilarious. What's Peter up to now?" Dick slung his arm around Laurie's shoulder and propped his chin on the top of her head.

Woody's Roast had been going on for more than an hour now, and the antics were getting really wild. Laurie thought *out of hand* was a better term for it. Already she had found trails of Kim's shrimp hors d'oeuvres in the crevices of the white leather sofa. A few minutes ago an ominous crash followed by a peal of raucous laughter upstairs had practically made her faint. She remained firmly planted in a corner of the rec-room-turned-banquet-hall, not even wanting to know who had broken what and what disaster lurked upstairs. She'd find out later.

But then a merry peal of laughter rose from the front of the room.

"Ladies, gentlemen, and of course, Woody!" Peter addressed the crowd in a dramatically formal tone. "As you know, every roast is crowned with a special event. A symbol, a gesture." Peter waved his hand broadly, bopping Woody on the nose.

"Hey, that's my only nose!" Woody groaned. He sat at the center of the table looking red-faced and humble and not entirely sure that all this attention was his cup of tea. "And, really, I've had enough 'events.' Isn't it time for our video?" he asked, uncomfortably eyeing the pile of gag gifts surrounding him: chartreuse suspenders, a whoopie cushion, a special edition of the *Woodpecker News*, courtesy of Sasha, Dee, and Karen. They had compiled a list of Woody's worst jokes, created fictitious interviews with the various Woody personas, collected childhood anecdotes from Phoebe, and searched *The Red and the Gold*'s files for particularly rakish photos of him. Then they had their printer run off a mini-edition of a souvenir paper. Brian Pierson had put together a tape of people groaning at Woody's puns, then laid down the sound over the background noise of Phoebe and Michael snapping several pairs of suspenders stretched over a washboard in a definite syncopated rhythm. "My cup runneth over, and out and around and under the table!" Woody joked, hoping desperately that no one was going to give him anything else. "I'm going to need a wheelbarrow to get this stuff home!"

"Ah!" Peter jumped off the table and whacked Woody on the back. "A wheelbarrow. The least we can do for our favorite punster, showman, and single-handed booster club, is present him with a — "

Everyone chimed in with Peter. "A WHEEL-BARROW!"

"Oh, no!" Woody buried his face in his hands, afraid to see what was coming next.

"Oh, no!" Laurie cried. "You guys aren't really bringing a wheelbarrow into my — "

Laurie was cut off as the lights went out. Several surprised cries and shrieks rang out. Voices shouting confused instructions filled the dark. Then a thump was heard on the patio, and the lights came back on. Ted and Bart wheeled in a large red wheelbarrow holding an enormous fake cake covered with crepe paper. Peter reached over to the stereo and flicked it on. French cancan music blared through the room. Kim squealed with laughter.

"I think I know what's coming next, and I don't want to see it!" Monica groaned as the boys steered the wheelbarrow directly in front of the table. Very carefully they lifted the cake out and set it before a very embarrassed Woody.

Over the blaring music he read the brightly painted inscription aloud: "TO OUR FAVORITE

CLASS CLOWN. WITHOUT YOU FOUR YEARS OF KENNEDY WOULD HAVE BEEN BLUE, BLUE, BLUE!"

No sooner were the words out of his mouth than the cake started moving. Fiona Stone and Katie Crawford jumped out. Fiona was dressed in a black-and-white harlequin outfit, her pretty face smeared with white greasepaint, dark circles painted around her eyes. Katie's red pigtails bounced out from beneath a perky patchwork clown hat. She wore a clown's ruffle-collared costume; she leaped off the table and cartwheeled about the room while Fiona danced a goofy dance right in front of Woody's place. Phoebe, Holly, and Bart lined up in front of Woody. Phoebe produced a wrinkled piece of paper from the pocket of her cub scout shirt. "One-two-three," she counted, then all three began singing a jingle Phoebe had just finished writing that afternoon. It more or less went to the tune of the cancan.

> "Woody Webster
> You're our favorite hero
> Meatball, Sausage, Pepper
> Hold the Onion, Extra Cheese.
>
> We will miss you
> When our school days are through
> Though your puns and pranks do
> Drive us crazy, nuts, and mad
>
> Your suspenders
> Are the living enders
> But so we don't offend yer
> This is the ending of this song!"

The whole room burst into wild applause.

Woody himself leaped onto the table and wrapped one arm around Fiona, one around Katie, and hugged them both. Then he reached down and pulled Phoebe up next to him. "What did I do to deserve this?" he bellowed, scrunching his face in a comical expression. "What did I do to deserve such friends!" He looked around the room, his grin stretching from ear to ear.

Brenda slipped in the side door and let her eyes adjust to the dimly lighted room. She looked around quickly, holding her breath. Brad wasn't there.

The noisy part of the Roast was over. The presentation of Jeremy and Karen's Video Yearbook had already begun, and Bart Einerson's rugged face filled the wall-sized TV screen. As Brenda made her way over to the sofa and dropped down next to Chris, she wondered how much she had missed.

"I'm so glad you came!" Chris whispered. Brenda merely nodded. She was glad, too, and knowing Brad hadn't turned up certainly made being there easier. When she left Garfield that afternoon, coming to Woody's Roast tonight was the last thing she wanted to do. But Chris had talked her into it. Whatever happened between her and Brad, she knew that Sasha, Phoebe, Woody, Janie, and everyone in the crowd were still her friends. Tonight's gathering was a very special time. Woody had made them all laugh so much. It seemed wrong to miss out on the tribute and sit home crying.

Brenda gladly accepted the soda Greg brought

over to her and leaned back in the couch watching the screen. After Bart's somewhat hokey talk about the Wild West and cowboys, Janie came on. Then Henry, Ted, and Peter. Brenda sat forward, entranced by the images of all her good friends, sharing their dreams, some familiar, some she never knew they had had.

She had forgotten all about Brad being an honorary part of the yearbook until Sasha's boyfriend, Rob, appeared on the screen. Like Brad, he was as much a part of that year's senior class as the rest of the crowd, even though he was in college and had never attended Kennedy High. Brenda steeled herself.

Chris squeezed her hand as Brad came on. Brenda thought she sensed some tension in the room. Everyone knew by now that Brad and she had had a pretty big fight. No one, except Chris, knew how it had finally ended this afternoon.

Brenda squelched the impulse to run out of the house. Brad's determined face looking right at her from the big screen sent an eerie shiver down her spine. Would she ever see him again? As he began to answer Karen's probing questions, Brenda found herself growing calm with the effort of quietly listening. Brad made his future sound so simple, so predictable. His whole life sounded like a series of steps, one leading neatly to the next: college, med school, starting a practice. There was nothing new here, nothing she didn't know about Brad. But Brenda was looking at him with new eyes. The differences she sensed between them weren't little things, crumbs to be swept under a carpet. They were as big and as insurmountable as she'd discovered that afternoon. Nothing could change that now.

Her own interview came on next. She had been nervous the afternoon Jeremy filmed it. She had been worried about Brad, worried about being late for the session at Garfield, frightened about her exam. Brenda cringed watching her videotaped image shift in the ugly upholstered chair, tug at her skirt, endlessly toy with her hair. As she answered Karen's questions she seemed so emotional, so full of movement. So opposite from Brad. That their love had lasted as long as it had seemed like some sort of miracle. Brenda choked back a sob and crept silently out of the room. Only when she was out on the patio did she let the tears flow.

She leaned her head against the white-shingled wall and gazed through her tears at the stars. She felt so empty, so alone, and, in spite of the warm night, so very cold.

# *Chapter*
# *17*

Brenda slapped down the snooze alarm for the third time that morning and pulled the covers over her head. Not that she was really sleeping. All night long she had wished and prayed she would fall asleep, but she had only tossed and turned on the wrinkled sheets, unable to get the list of chemical formulas and terms out of her head. It seemed rather ironic that her brain was stuffed with what would become, after today, absolutely useless information.

Of course, if Brenda had been really sure she'd never take chemistry again, she would have slept like a log. She rolled over on her back and wondered exactly how a log did sleep. Too bad chemistry didn't teach her useful facts like that. She smothered a yawn with her hand and peered through the muslin printed sheet up at the ceiling. The morning sun danced through the spaces on the sides of her window shade and bathed her room in a bright, uncomfortably white light. Mornings, Brenda thought, particularly mornings of chemistry finals, should be banned forever. She lay there thinking how much she preferred the night. Especially summer nights; they were soft and starry now and so pleasantly warm. Tears slowly welled up in her eyes. That didn't surprise her. Every day now she had woken up crying, knowing there'd be a whole summer ahead of nights without Brad.

"Brenda, the shower's free!" Chris yelled down the hall. Brenda swung her legs out of bed and rubbed the tears from her eyes with the sleeve of her nightgown. Chris was definitely a morning person, Brenda thought irritably as she reached for her robe. She walked over to the mirror and stared at her face. Her usually clear skin looked pale and blotchy, and dark circles ringed her huge eyes. She combed her hair back with her fingers, and made a face. "At least you *look* like you've been studying. That should count for something in McQuarrie's book." She made her way to the shower, trying to put aside all thoughts of Brad, trying to organize the jumble of scientific facts she had crammed into her head over the past few days.

When she arrived at school, the flowers tucked in the door of her locker surprised her. She stopped halfway down the hall and just stared. For a moment all her fears of failing, of not graduating, evaporated. "Brad!" she murmured, then pushed her way through the crowd and reached for the bouquet. Slowly, she unfolded the note. But when she saw the writing, she found it wasn't from Brad at all.

*I'm not going to wish you luck. I* know *you can do it, and I expect an invitation to your graduation.*

                                                            *Kara.*

Matt, Pam, and Tony had signed the note, too, each scrawling a short message. No matter what happened on the exam, she would treasure the note forever. Knowing her friends were behind her right now meant a lot. They were each an important part of the life she'd chosen for herself, and she loved them for that.

*"Brenda! Brenda Austin!"* Chris screeched four days later as she spotted her sister descending the stairs toward the gym. School was over for the day, and the halls were packed. Half of Kennedy stared in disbelief as the usually composed student body president tore down the hall toward her sister.

Brenda paused with her hand on the banister, Janie right beside her. "What's the matter?" Janie wondered. "I hope it's not bad news," she added with a worried look.

Brenda hoped not, either, and ran down the remaining stairs to meet her sister. "What happened?" Brenda cried, then breathed a sigh of relief. Chris's expression left no doubt her news was good news.

"Come with me, just come with me." Chris grabbed Brenda's arm and steered her past the goups of curious students to the bulletin board hanging on the wall outside the gym. Janie followed close behind them.

"Chris — " Brenda protested.

"Look, silly, just look!" Chris tapped the cork surface with her finger and bounced up and down on her toes.

At first the information didn't register. A list of names, letters after them. No, not letters. Grades. Brenda's heart stopped. She forced herself to look at the top of the first column. As usual her named appeared first. With a trembling hand she traced a line from her name to the letter grade opposite. "B+," she gasped. That was impossible. She quickly checked the top of the paper. This had to be for some other course. Her mouth fell open. "Chris!" she cried. "I got a B+ in my chemistry final!" Then she threw her arms around her sister and started laughing and crying all at once. "Do you believe it!" she whooped, throwing her books, her bag, and her gymsuit up toward the ceiling. "I actually passed the course! I'm going to graduate! And I'm going to be the first senior across that stage to get my diploma, and no one, *no one,* is going to be happier about graduating than me."

"Congratulations!" Janie cheered from behind them.

"I'm surprised you didn't notice earlier!" Bart walked up smiling. "The grades have been posted for a couple of hours now." He hugged Brenda and turned to Chris. "You're wanted in Beman's office. Some problem's cropped up with the graduation programs and the printer."

"Ooooh," Chris groaned. "Why did I ever sign up for that ceremony committee." Before she started down the hall, she gave Brenda's hand a firm squeeze. "Let's do something special tonight. Let's celebrate!"

"You're on!" Brenda said, flashing her sister a thumbs-up sign.

"Oh, there you are!" Pamela Green struggled through the crowd to Brenda's side. "I've been looking all over for you. I heard about the test. Congratulations."

Brenda smiled but considered Pam's face carefully. "Is something wrong?"

"Yes," Pamela said, lowering her voice and taking Brenda aside. "It's Kara. Tony said it was a real emergency. You'd better come with me to Garfield right away."

Brenda's face whitened. "But she's been doing so well lately. . . ."

"I know," Pamela said, guiding Brenda toward the exit. "Listen, I'll give you a ride; I borrowed Matt's car. He — uh — he stayed behind to help Tony."

Brenda hurried alongside Pam, wondering what could have happened. Pamela seemed very confused, as if she couldn't quite get the facts of her story straight. Brenda thought of the time one of the Garfield residents had flipped and gotten very abusive toward Pam. Thanks to Tony and Matt she hadn't gotten hurt; but she had been pretty shaken up, almost quitting her job as a volunteer art teacher. Remembering that, Brenda doubled her pace and reached Matt's Camaro before Pam had taken out her key. "Pamela, you seem very upset," she said firmly, walking over to the driver's side. "Let me drive."

Pamela looked at her as if she were crazy, then nodded. "Okay, you're right. I'm too worked up right now. I don't know how I made it here in one piece." Pamela handed Brenda the keys and meekly deposited herself in the passenger seat.

"Do you want to talk about it?" Brenda asked gently as they pulled into the beginning of rush hour traffic.

Pam looked out the window and dismally shook her head. She pressed her hand to her forehead and said glumly, "You know it's too bad all this had to happen now. Kara was doing so well, and this — well — it's just terrible. It's such a downer, just when everyone was so up about getting ready for the graduation party. Of all things to happen. . . ." Pam's voice trailed off in a sigh. She pulled a tissue out of her bag and blew her nose loudly, then turned back to the window and gave a few lingering, weepy sniffs.

Brenda struggled to remain patient. Pamela had said how terrible "it" was. But Brenda still didn't have a clue what had happened. She felt like shaking Pam until the information spilled out of her. Some people, Brenda reflected in annoyance, just aren't good in emergencies. They fall apart. She hadn't suspected Pamela was that sort, but it took the acid test of a real crisis at Garfield to see what someone was made of.

She parked at the curb, and before Pamela

had a chance to open the passenger door, Brenda raced up the front steps of Garfield House. She flung open the door.

*"Surprise!"*

Brenda blinked. "What's going on?" It took a minute to sink in. The worried frown on her forehead vanished. Her cheeks flushed crimson. "I don't believe this. Is this a party? For me?" Her voice, usually so low and husky, came out as a squeak. She sank back against the wall and slipped down to the floor, not knowing if she was about to laugh or cry.

Pamela stood in the doorway, doubled over with laughter. Matt walked up to her and enveloped her in a hug. "I thought she was going to kill me." Pamela recounted her efforts of trying to convince Brenda something had happened to Kara. "She was so upset, I couldn't give her the details. I couldn't even make something up. I was so confused," she gasped, wiping tears of laughter from her eyes.

Tony walked over to Brenda. He grabbed one hand, Matt the other, and they pulled her to her feet. Brenda couldn't remember ever being so embarrassed, or flattered, in her whole life. "But why me? Why a party for me? What happened to the graduation party?" Brenda wondered, looking around. The decorations she and Pam and some of the art students had made were hanging from the ceiling and the walls. "This is your party stuff, not mine!" she exclaimed, looking at Don Amtson and Marcia Weiss, two of Garfield's seniors.

"This is a party for you because you practically

168

aced that exam," Kara crowed from behind the pool table. It was covered with a bright paper cloth and piled high with plates of food and stacks of soda cans. "And because you're graduating, too. And because you're part of Garfield."

Brenda looked at Kara. The girl seemed transformed. Her mousy hair looked shiny and full, and her small, round face was pink with pride. She was wearing a soft peasant blouse over her jeans, and the silvery blue color set off her gray eyes. Brenda impulsively walked to her side and gave her a warm hug. "Then, this party's for you, too," Brenda said quietly. "Because without you, Kara, I wouldn't have made it through that final."

# *Chapter*
# *18*

"To conclude, I would like to paraphrase a poem our newspaper editor, Sasha Jenkins, once shared with me, four years ago, one late spring afternoon on the steps of the Kennedy Playhouse. The poet's words express far better than my own the true spirit of this class as it passes on through the portals of Kennedy High, bearing one burden of dreams, hopes, and responsibilities, into the world.

"The doors in my life are not exits but entrances, and I begin at last to be brave, to slowly one by one, step through."

As she concluded her valedictorian speech, Chris's voice was charged with restrained emotion. For a long moment absolute silence filled the auditorium. Then, almost as one, the entire audience leaped to its feet and applauded furiously. Brenda's eyes shone as she looked at her sister. Chris gave a stiff little bow and pushed the golden tassel on her mortarboard out of her face. She shook Principal Beman's hand, then descended the stairs and made her way to Brenda's side.

"Incredible," Brenda whispered, wiping the tears from her eyes. "That was beautiful, Chris."

Chris pressed her hand as Principal Beman stepped up to the mike. "I've never been so nervous in all my life," she groaned, brushing a stray wisp of hair off her face. The auditorium was stifling, and the rattle of paper as people fanned themselves with their programs practically drowned out the principal's next announcement.

"And now, for the conferring of diplomas. Will the graduating seniors please stand up."

Brenda swallowed hard. Her knees were shaking. All week long she had dreaded this moment. Thanks to her name she'd be the first to walk up those four formidable steps, cross the broad stage, take the diploma, and remember to shake the principal's hand.

"Brenda Austin!" he boomed into the mike.

Brenda took a first tentative step into the aisle. She straightened her shoulders and walked carefully up the stairs, praying she wouldn't trip in her black high heels. From the far side of the stage, she glimpsed the diploma, a bright red ribbon wrapped around the middle. All at once her fear evaporated. She walked, almost ran, toward the principal, her blue gown flying open to reveal the white drop-waist dress she wore beneath. Brenda stuck out her hand with a broad

171

smile. When her fingers closed around the treasured piece of paper, she had to catch her breath. To Principal Beman's amazement, she cried "I did it!" and reached up and planted a kiss on his cheek. The whole room started cheering as Brenda practically flew across the stage and down the opposite side while Chris walked, laughing, in her wake.

The bonfire was raging on the banks of the Potomac, and Phoebe stood in the silent circle of seniors gathered around it, hugging a shadowy bundle to her chest. The round of graduation parties was over, and it was time for the passing-on ceremony. During the graduation night bonfire at Potomac Park, each senior would toss a prized possession — one that symbolized the best of their life at Kennedy High — into the flames. Until tonight Phoebe had thought it was a pretty dumb custom, certainly not something worth giving too much attention to. She would toss in her three-ring looseleaf binder, the one she'd had for almost four years, with the purple plastic cover plastered with decals of places she'd never been to.

But during Chris's speech this afternoon something had happened to Phoebe. She had been listening closely to Chris, drinking in every word. Not just because she was proud of her best friend, but because Chris's emotional statement about graduation being an entrance, not an exit, had stirred Phoebe to the depths of her soul. All at once she understood the meaning of the ceremony planned for that evening. Only one thing she owned symbolized leaving behind the happiest years of her life so far, moving on to what she knew now would be an even more wonderful era. And it wasn't her purple looseleaf binder.

Now, someone, Woody or Bart, began humming the Kennedy Fight Song, softly and slowly. Soon everyone joined in. It sounded so sad and meaningful, more like a dirge than a call to action. First Peter stepped up to the fire carrying a record album. The cover was worn and frayed, and in the flickering light Phoebe made out the title and stifled a gasp: Springsteen's *Born in the USA*. Peter tossed it into the flames, and Phoebe watched in horror as the cardboard cover wrinkled up, baring the melting black disc inside. Ted stepped up next. From the circle of juniors behind her, Phoebe heard a loud sniff. It was Molly. Phoebe focused her attention back on Ted in time to see him throw a baseball into the flames. "He hit his first home run with that!" Molly whispered in the dark. Chris sacrificed her favorite pair of penny loafers; Monica, an old stuffed yellow dog with one eye missing; Bart, his old Stetson; Woody, his best red suspenders; Laurie, her heart-shaped plastic Candy Hearts bag; and Michael, a warped but beloved old bow for his cello.

Then Brenda stepped out of the shadows, and Phoebe watched her slowly approach the fire. In her black jeans and dark tank top she looked almost like a silhouette before the dancing flames. Her back was toward Phoebe, so she couldn't see her face, but she gasped as Brenda reached up toward her neck. For a moment Phoebe feared Brenda was going to take off the beautiful tur-

173

quoise earring Brad had given her and throw it in, but instead Brenda pulled off the small triangle cloth, tied loosely about her throat. Just before Brenda dropped it into the blaze, Phoebe recognized it as Brad's worn blue bandanna. He had given it to Brenda once when they were hiking over the summer to tie back her hair. Brenda stood silently watching the flames consume the frayed cotton. Then she stepped back into the shadows. As she passed, Phoebe impulsively squeezed her hand. Brenda squeezed back and then slipped away into the park, away from the fire.

Then it was Phoebe's turn. She stepped forward cautiously, holding back tears. She squeezed her bundle tightly before giving it up. This was something that couldn't be undone. She looked up and caught Michael's eye. He was standing across the fire from her, an encouraging smile on his face. Phoebe forced herself to keep her eyes open. "Good-bye!" she whispered, pressing the soft fabric to her cheeks. Then with a brave whoop she hurled her worn pink overalls into the blaze. They landed flat, dead center, sprawling like an old rag doll. For a moment she was powerless to turn away. She felt an odd fascination watching first the right leg burn, then the left strap. But finally the tears came, blinding her, and she ran off sobbing.

Chris materialized by her side. "Oh, Phoebe!" Chris cried, throwing her arms around her friend. Chris was crying, too; everyone was. Then everyone was hugging everyone else in a big huddle with Phoebe and Chris in the middle. Suddenly

Chris met Phoebe's eye and started laughing. Phoebe started laughing, too. Then the two of them broke down in hysterical, uncontrollable giggles, for just the joy of it — the same way they had been laughing together ever since junior high. "Phoebe, you are the most wonderful person in the whole world!" Chris declared joyously. And finally, to Phoebe, being called a wonderful person didn't sound so bad.

Jonathan's dog, Sherlock, sniffed out a trail in the dark, winding toward the bonfire, then back along the narrow walk, his tail wagging furiously. Brenda lay on a bench beneath a lamp on the path, looking up at the fading stars. As the friendly hound passed by, she reached down and tickled him behind his droopy ears. He paused and happily licked her bare ankles, then continued on his way into the pine grove along the banks of the river. When he was gone, Brenda sighed. She suddenly felt very alone. It wasn't a bad feeling, though. She just felt sad. So much had ended over the past few days. High school, her life at Kennedy, Brad.

Brenda sat up and folded her legs underneath her, tugging down her sleek black tank top. The night was warm, but a light predawn breeze blew in from the river. She chafed her bare arms and thought of how sad Brad had looked earlier that evening. She had seen him at Jonathan Preston's house, then over at Bart and Diana's, and finally at Laurie's. They had done a good job of avoiding each other; it had been easy in the crowd. He had turned up with some college friends and hung out mostly with Ted and Molly. There had been enough commotion all evening to keep their friends from feeling embarrassed or awkward about the two of them being in the same room not talking.

She gave a little shiver. Looking toward the fire, Brenda watched couples pairing off. Again she sighed. Her relationship with Brad was over. Someday things would begin again with someone else. Brenda knew that. She also knew it would take a long time. She had never loved anyone quite like she had loved Brad.

A figure stepped out of the shadow of the woods. Brenda straightened up and glanced back toward the bonfire. She got up, intending to run down the dimly lighted path toward the safety of the crowd. The figure took one step closer, then another.

Brenda stayed rooted to the spot. She didn't have to see his face to know. It was Brad. She still had the chance to go back and join her friends. But she didn't want to. Too much had passed between them to just walk off, pretending, as she had all night, that she just didn't know him anymore.

He approached, hands in his pockets, his proud shoulders slightly stooped. He gave her a long searching look and finally said, "I felt it shouldn't end this way between us." As usual Brad was being honest, direct.

"But it has ended," Brenda said with a firmness that surprised her.

Brad winced slightly as if in pain. "I love you too much to let it end so badly. I still don't agree

with your decision — about school and all that
— but I respect what you're doing. I came here
to tell you that." He stopped, waiting for Brenda
to respond. His dark eyes were kind, expectant.
He wanted something to happen between them.
He wanted her back.

Brenda steeled herself and averted his eyes.
"I — I appreciate that, Brad. I know how hard
it is. I said some unfair things, too." Unable to
find words to express her feelings, Brenda looked
up. The way Brad was gazing at her sent a familiar shot of warmth up her spine. It was so power-
ful, Brenda couldn't resist anymore. "Oh,
Brad — " she cried. Then his arms were around
her. His hands ran through her wild tangled hair,
and he showered her face, her neck, her hands,
with kisses.

"I love you so much," he whispered, stopping
his kisses long enough to catch his breath. Then
he drew her face toward his and pressed his lips
to hers.

Brenda abandoned herself to his embrace,
wrapping her arms around his neck and holding
on to him as if she would never let go. "Brenda,
Brenda," he murmured into her ear. "Please, let's
try again. Brenda and Brad, take four. We can
make it work. I know we can." His words sounded
like a prayer.

For a second more, Brenda continued to hold
him. How she wanted to say, Yes, let's try again.
But she knew it wouldn't work. Slowly she pulled
back from his touch and dropped her hands to
her sides. "No, Brad," she said, her voice trembling. The wind blew her hair across her face,

177

and she swept it out of her eyes and met Brad's gaze. "It can't work. For all the reasons we talked about. We're going in two different directions." Her voice was barely audible. They stood there in silence, not touching, for what seemed like a very long time.

From somewhere down by the river Brenda heard the first notes of a bird's song. Brad heard it, too. Together they turned and looked at the water. It shimmered with the light of a new day. The pale gray sky over the east bank was pink now, and the golden rim of the sun was just visible over the tips of the trees. Instinctively Brenda reached for Brad's hand. When she turned to face him, tears streaked her face. She stood on tiptoe and kissed him one last time, sweetly and tenderly. "I'll always love you, Brad. And I'll never forget you."

Brad's eyes filled with tears. "So, it's really the end." He looked at Brenda one last time, then turned around. She watched him walk down the long winding path into the woods.

Over the music of the dawn birds, Brenda murmured the last words of Chris's speech aloud. " 'The doors in my life are not exits but entrances, and I begin at last to be brave, to slowly one by one, step through.' "

# COUPLES

Coming Soon . . .
**Couples Special Edition**
*BEACH PARTY!*

It had all started when Jeremy produced a beach ball. Blown up, it was fully two feet in diameter, but so light that he could easily throw it twenty feet into the air. A game of catch had turned into keep-away, and the first time the ball sailed into the water, they had all raced after it.

"Shirts against skins," Woody had shouted. That got a laugh from everybody.

"You wish," Fiona had replied smartly.

Someone suggested "Boys against the girls," and the next thing Pamela knew, Ben had passed her the beach ball, and the other girls were cheering. Michael struggled to his feet and reached for it, but she passed it to Fiona. Fiona paused just long enough to stick out her tongue at the other team, then calmly dunked the ball for the winning point.

"Boo!" Jonathan called through cupped hands. "Boo! Fix! Forrest took a dive," he continued loudly. "He threw the game!"

Ben crouched down and leaped at Jonathan, who stepped deftly aside and let him do a belly-flop. As if on signal, everyone was splashing water at everyone else, laughing like hyenas all the while.

Ben quickly came to Pamela's defense. Throwing himself in front of her, he began to splash Jonathan. When Jonathan finally escaped, Ben turned around quickly, sending himself and Pamela tumbling into the waves. Practically choking she was laughing so hard, she reached for Ben's outstretched hand and let him pull her to her feet until she was in his arms. She could feel her heart pounding. It felt so natural to stand so close to someone this way. To someone . . . someone who *wasn't* Matt Jacobs.

She pressed her palms against Ben's chest and leaned back to look into his eyes. He looked back uncertainly and seemed as confused by their embrace as she was. He gave her a flickering half-smile, inviting her to pretend with him that they were simply playing some sort of game. But they both knew better. Whatever was happening, wherever it might lead, this was obviously no game.

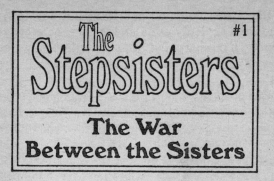

# The Stepsisters

#1

## The War Between the Sisters

*by Tina Oaks*

## Chapter Excerpt

Paige Whitman unzipped the plastic cover that held the dress she was to wear to her father's wedding. She had put off looking at the dress until the very last minute. When she learned the dress would be pink, she had groaned. There were colors she loved, colors she could take or leave alone, and then there was pink, which hated her as much as she hated it!

And the style was as impossible for her as the color. She didn't even have to try the dress on to know how it would look. At sixteen she was taller than most of her friends, and thinner without being really skinny. But taller meant longer, and she knew her neck was too long to wear a low, rounded neckline like that.

Paige's instinct was to wail. Dresses were supposed to do things *for* you, not *to* you. The only tiny comforting thing she could think of was that Katie Summer Guthrie, her fifteen-year-old step-sister-to-be would be wearing a matching monstrosity. Even though pink was a blonde's color, not even Katie could look like anything in *that* dress. It was comforting that she wouldn't be alone in her humiliation.

Beyond the other bed in the hotel room they shared, Paige's ten-year-old sister Megan hummed happily as she put on her own dress. Megan was a naturally happy-go-lucky girl, but Paige had never seen her as excited as she had been since their father announced his coming marriage to Virginia Mae Guthrie. Her father had tried to control his own excitement and tell them about his bride-to-be in a calm, sensible way. But Paige knew him too well to be fooled, and anyway he gave himself dead away!

He started by telling them how he had met Virginia Mae on a business trip to Atlanta, then how beautiful she was. He went from that to her divorce five years before and how she had been raising her three children alone ever since. Paige almost giggled. Here was William Whitman, whose logic and cool courtroom delivery were legendary in Philadelphia legal circles. Yet he was jumping around from one subject to another as he talked about Virginia Mae.

Paige had driven down to Atlanta with her father and Megan earlier in the summer so the children could meet. Paige had to agree that Virginia Mae Guthrie was as lovely as she was gentle. ·

Paige had tried to shrug away the twinge of resentment that came when she thought of Katie Summer. The girl had to be putting on an act. *Nobody* could possibly be as lighthearted and happy as she pretended to be. And nobody would be that pretty in a fair world. Seventeen-year-old Tucker seemed like a nice enough guy, although his exaggerated good manners threw Paige off a little. Ten-year-old Mary Emily was cute. But it was awkward to be the only one holding back when her father and Megan were both so obviously deliriously happy.

Her father made the marriage plans sound so simple: "Right after our wedding, Virginia and the children will move up here to Philadelphia. We'll all be one big happy family together."

Paige had said nothing then or since, but concealing her doubts hadn't made them go away. She hated feeling like a sixteen-year-old grouch, but it just didn't make sense that everything would work out that easily. Not only would there be more than twice as many people in the same house as before, but the people themselves would be different.

Even if people from the south didn't think differently than people from the north, they certainly *sounded* different when they talked. And the Guthries were as completely southern as Paige's family was northern. Mrs. Guthrie and her three children had lived in Atlanta all their lives.

Megan giggled and fluffed out her full skirt. "Isn't it great? I can't wait to show this dress back home."

Back home. Philadelphia meant only one person to Paige . . . Jake Carson. She shuddered at the thought of Jake seeing her in that pink dress. She would die, just simply die where she stood, if he ever saw her looking this gross.

She sighed and fiddled with the neck of the pink dress, wishing she hadn't even thought of Jake. Simply running his name through her mind was enough to sweep her with those familiar waves of almost physical pain. It didn't make sense that loving anyone could be so painful. But just the memory of his face, his intense expression, the brooding darkness of his thoughtful eyes was enough to destroy her self-control.

But even when Jake looked at her, he was absolutely blind to who she really was. She knew what he thought: that she was a nice kid, that she was fun to talk to, that she was William Whitman's daughter. Period. He didn't give the slightest indication that he even realized that she was a girl, much less a girl who loved him with such an aching passion that she couldn't meet his eyes for fear he might read her feelings there.

Megan caught Paige around the waist and clung to her. "Sometimes I get scared, thinking about the changes. It *is* going to be wonderful, isn't it, Paige?" Megan's voice held the first tremulous note of doubt Paige had heard from her sister.

"Absolutely wonderful," Paige assured her, wishing she felt as much confidence as she put into her tone.

Even as she spoke, she saw Jake's face again, his dark eyes intent on hers as he had talked to her about the wedding. "Look at your dad," Jake had said. "Anything that makes him that happy has to be a lucky break for all of you."

She had nodded, more conscious of how lucky she was to be with Jake than anything else.

Jake had worked around their house in Philadelphia for about a year and a half. Paige didn't believe in love at first sight, but it had almost been that way with her. From the first day, she found herself waiting breathlessly for the next time he came to work. She found herself remembering every word he said to her, turning them over and over in her mind later. It wasn't that he was mysterious. It was more that she always had the sense of there being so much more in his mind than he was saying. She was curious about him, his life, his friends, how he thought about things. In contrast to a lot of people who smiled easily and laughed or hummed when they worked, he was silent and withdrawn unless he was talking with someone.

Before he came, she hadn't realized how painful it was to love someone the way she did Jake. She hadn't asked to fall in love with him or anybody. She had even tried desperately to convince herself that he wasn't different from other boys, just nicer and older. That didn't work because it wasn't true. Jake really was different from the boys she knew at school. Although he talked enough when he had something to say, he was mostly a little aloof without being awkward and shy. And he wasn't an ordinary kind of handsome. His features were strong, with firm cheekbones; deeply set eyes; and a full, serious mouth.

Maybe one day she would quit loving him as quickly as she had begun. But even thinking about that happening brought a quick thump of panic in her chest. Knowing how it felt to be so much in love, how could she bear to live without it?

Later, when the wedding march began and the doors of the little chapel were opened, Paige was overwhelmed with the strange feeling that she was watching all this from a distance. Even as she walked beside Katie Summer and kept careful time to the music, she didn't feel as if she was a part of what was happening.

Paige felt a touch against her arm and looked over at Katie Summer. Katie flashed her a quick, sly smile that brought a fleeting dimple to her cheek. Paige swallowed hard, ducked her head, and looked away. Later she would have to deal with this girl, but not now, not while her father was repeating the same vows he had made so many years before to her own mother.

But that quick glance had been enough to remind her of how wrong she had been about how Katie Summer would look in her matching pink dress. It made Paige feel leggy and graceless beside her.

All the Guthries were good-looking. Tucker was almost as tall as Paige's father, and comfortingly nice to look at in a different, curly-haired way. Mary Emily, behind with Megan, was button cute. But the girl at Paige's side was just too much! Katie's thick, dark blonde curls spilled in glorious profusion around her glowing face.

Her pink dress picked up the rosiness of her deep tan and showed off the sparkle of her laughing blue eyes. Paige held her head high, fighting a sudden feeling of inadequacy that made her breath come short.

Looking back, Paige was sure that the wedding brunch was as beautiful as any meal she would ever eat. As they ate, Grandma Summer bent to Paige to make conversation, her soft voice rising in an exciting, different rhythm. "Virginia Mae tells me you play the piano, Paige, and that you're an excellent student. My, I know your father is just *so* proud of you."

Before Paige could reply, Katie flipped her glowing head of curls, turned away, and put her hand on Paige's father's arm. "I just had a perfectly *terrifying* thought," she said, looking up into his face. "My goodness, I hope you don't expect *me* to have a lot of talents or be a bookworm. I've got to tell you right off that I don't believe in all that."

After an astonished look, Paige's father covered Katie's hand with his, and chuckled. "That's pretty interesting," he said. "What *do* you believe in, Katie Summer?"

Her laugh was quick and soft. "Having a *wonderful* time, just like I am today."

Naturally he beamed at her. Who could help it when everything she said sounded so intimate and appealing in that soft, coaxing drawl? Paige felt a shiver of icy jealousy. That Katie Summer was something else!